CW00880825

DAF

A PRELUDE

JILL BRETHERTON

DARKMERE

A PRELUDE

Matador
9 De Montfort Mews
Leicester LE1 7FW, UK
Tel: (+44) 116 255 9311 / 9312
Email: books@troubador.co.uk
Web: www.troubador.co.uk/matador

ISBN 978 1906510 077

A Cataloguing-in-Publication (CIP) catalogue record for this book
is available from the British Library.

Mixed Sources
Product group from well-managed
forests and other controlled sources
www.fsc.org Cert no. TT-COC-2082
© 1996 Forest Stewardship Council

Typeset in 11pt Stempel Garamond by Troubador Publishing Ltd, Leicester, UK
Printed in the UK by The Cromwell Press Ltd, Trowbridge, Wilts, UK

Matador is an imprint of Troubador Publishing Ltd

For Eleanor, Elizabeth and Evelyn
Thank you for being so utterly wonderful in every way.

And

For Carolyn and Gwyn
Thanks will never be enough.

1

CHRISTMAS EVE

*I*man Khan had stopped running. She was panting doubled over with her hands on her hips waiting for the stitch to pass. She could think of better places to find herself on Christmas Eve. It was dark and she was lost. The crummy backstreet that she found herself in was at the back of a fast food outlet and was piled high with filthy detritus bursting from bins. The bricks around her were decorated with graffiti. She did not understand the meaning of the words nor did she care, she was concentrating on the three young men who were approaching her.

Damn it, she should have let that guy run off with her purse. Why did she have to chase him? Now he was gone and she was stuck in a dead end, cornered by three drunken wasters who thought they were God's gift to women. They were not God's gift to her and she needed to escape but how?

"Hey lady!" the leader of the pack was stumbling towards her now. "Hey, beautiful lady, want some festive fun?"

"How would you like a broken neck?" she answered as though she were unafraid.

The man stopped. "Ooh, fiery, I like it. Say where d'ya get that sexy accent from?"

"Hell," she answered.

The man was suddenly angry, "Hey lady, you need to learn to be a little more friendly."

He was getting closer. She really was going to have to break his neck. That wouldn't be a problem but then what about the other two, she'd never taken on three before.

The man was close now, he lunged at her. She avoided him skilfully but she was backing herself closer to the wall, she was getting more and more trapped.

Suddenly a black saloon car screeched around the corner, the headlamps lighting up the misty rain. Her drunken assailant turned and faced the glare of the lights before jumping backwards out of its way. The car parted her from the drunk and the door flew open.

"Get in," a man ordered.

The woman looked from her assailant back to the shadowy face in the car. The three drunks were coming for her again, they were really pissed.

"Get in," the man ordered more forcefully. He was English.

She got in. Something came over her head and she was grabbed by both arms as the car screeched off. Before she knew it she was blindfolded and her arms were tied behind her back while she was searched for firearms. She had none.

"We have your bag. It is safe," the man said coldly.

"It was a set up," she gasped, cursing herself for being so easily tricked.

The Englishman didn't speak again. She tried quizzing him but he wouldn't be drawn. He was under orders she could tell but whose orders she wondered.

*

The car stopped. Iman estimated they had been driving for about two hours before she was ushered out into the cold night air. Still blindfolded, she was steered down some steps: she counted thirty. She heard the swish of a sliding door, then she was in an elevator, but the elevator was going down, down, down. There was a long straight walk along a corridor before she heard several beeps, a security measure of some description preceding the opening of the next door.

"We have the goods," she heard the Englishman say. There was no response, although she could hear another person moving. There was a click and some more beeps and then a prolonged, high pitched beep. A heavier door swished open, she knew the sort from the lab she worked at. This was real high security. She was really afraid by the time she was pushed into a room and her blindfold was removed.

"Miss Khan, welcome," said the President of the United States.

Iman didn't speak. She couldn't. She was staring down the long glossy mahogany table at the rich and powerful faces occupying all but one of the chairs. She recognised the two men sitting either side of the President. Professor Jim Ellis, a colleague employed by NASA and ...well the other man was a world superstar: the energy tycoon Levi Washington. His black face was as beautiful in real life as his photographs suggested, but his strange luminous green eyes were more piercing. Levi smiled a broad smile revealing his trademark gold tooth.

"Sit down Ms Khan," Levi said gesturing to the empty chair opposite.

The Englishman untied her before stepping back into the doorway as though guarding it. She could see the handle of his gun peeking out from his jacket. Cautiously she made her way down the long windowless room to the seat.

"Miss Khan, you may be wondering why you are here," said the President.

"That is an understatement," she replied coolly.

"Miss Khan, your extraordinary genius in the field of astrophysics and cosmology has been noticed. That is why you are here. You are here, we hope, to help us." The President smiled. Iman Khan did not return his smile but continued to eye him coolly.

"Ms Khan," Levi took over, she was a tough cookie, he was going to have to try hard with this one. "We need your help." His southern drawl was more noticeable than it had been in press interviews; he was putting it on, softening himself for effect, she wasn't stupid.

"We've been looking for something for a long, long time now and we just can't seem to find it."

"Really, try the sock drawer," she answered sarcastically, noticing that he was tapping a black file on the table in front of him.

There was a murmur of laughter although the tension in the room was unbearable.

"We would try the sock drawer," answered Levi, genuinely amused, "but we know it's not there because the thing we are looking for is up there," he pointed to the ceiling, "I mean out there, in space."

Again she made no comment and her face said nothing.

"We are looking for a Hole Ms Khan, a Hole in space."

"You want me to find a black Hole in space just like that? Did you have any particular black Hole in mind?" she asked sarcastically. "You know what you are asking is impossible."

Levi looked troubled: "Ms Khan this thing you're calling a black Hole isn't really a black Hole in the known scientific sense, it's more of a tear in space and time."

"You want me to find a tear in space?" She was not impressed.

"Yes maam," replied Levi beaming, "but there is also light. It is a special light that seeps out from the wound.

The light is a beacon." He let the implication of what he was saying hang in the air.

"What sort of light?" she asked warily.

Levi smiled. He knew from her answer that she was the right person. If she didn't already know something she would have told him that what he was saying was ridiculous, unheard of, scientifically impossible even. "The light that leaks from the tear should make the Hole easier to find," he finished.

"If you cannot find it what makes you think that I can?"

"You live, eat and breathe your work, your work is space," the President answered.

The President's summary of her work was a gross oversimplification. Under different circumstances she may have been offended but now she was silent, secretly panicking beneath her cool exterior. It was obvious they had been watching her, but for how long? What if they knew about her secret already? God no! But she didn't give her feelings away. She learned that much in the training camps.

"How will I find it?" She was blunt, to the point.

"Ms Khan if we knew that…" There was false laughter again.

"Why do you want to find it?"

"Because of this?" Levi opened the black file he'd been tapping and handed her a photocopy of an old etching.

Iman stared at the picture, absorbing the shocking

detail of mass human sacrifice. Hundreds of contorted, terrified bodies were being heaped down a large black Hole, while spectacular beams of light that looked like limbs with elongated fingers, wrapped themselves around the bodies, pulling them down into the darkness.

"What has this to do with space?" she added still cool despite the gut wrenching detail of horror.

"This Hole is in space currently but is due to reconnect with earth soon. We want to find it before anyone else does. If we can track it in space first…"

"This is nonsense," she wanted to appear sceptical.

"Is this nonsense?" Levi was pulling something from beneath his shirt. She drew back. He was going to threaten her with a gun.

It wasn't a gun but it burned her eyes so that she couldn't look at the thing that he had produced.

"Somebody get her a visor," Levi ordered.

A dark visor was placed over her eyes and she was able to open them again. Levi was holding a clear pendant. Tiny strands of light like golden snakes were coiled around inside squirming and vying for room, for space to stretch and beckon.

The President explained: "We found it in Iraq, near the site where we believe the Hole originally located itself last time it was here on earth. Jim?" he turned to the man on his left.

Jim Ellis took up the explanation: "The light is like

nothing we've ever encountered before. The properties of this light obey none of the known laws of physics. We do not understand anything about it. The only thing that we can be sure of is that it cannot be from this universe."

"If we can find evidence of this light in space we believe we can find the Hole," Levi concluded.

"You never did say why you wanted to find this Hole so much?" she asked. She was rattled.

"You don't think the picture explains?" The President was surprised by her question.

"Not really," she shrugged as though she was indifferent.

"Well," the President was perplexed, she really was a tough cookie. He had been warned but most people in the face of such powerful company couldn't do enough to help. The President looked to Levi for aid. Levi shrugged then nodded. The President cleared his throat. "The Hole leads to the afterlife," he answered sombrely.

"Heaven actually," added Levi smiling a broad satisfied smile and showing off his gold tooth. "The light is the link between the two worlds: a superhighway if you like, between life and the afterlife. If we get our hands on this Hole, we can control the gates to Heaven."

Iman was reeling. A trace of fear flashed across her face. It didn't go unnoticed but she recovered herself quickly. She wasn't going to tell them that she already knew the whereabouts of this light in space and that she'd been studying it for months, watching the magnificent tendrils of light reaching down to earth and pulling the black Hole along with it. She wasn't going to give up her secrets that easily.

"There are other scientists, more senior with more impressive track records, why me?" she pressed.

The President and Levi looked at each other cryptically and she felt the other members fidgeting uncomfortably as Levi opened the black file again. He pushed a photograph towards her. The photograph was of a painted portrait. The woman portrayed was a dark exotic beauty. Iman took a step back from the picture; it was the first time she looked visibly shaken.

"This portrait of you was found on the wall of a cave in Iraq," Levi began, "the portrait is approximately three and a half thousand years old."

"But... I don't understand... how... why?" she gasped.

Levi answered: "Because you are special," he said, "you are one of us."

4 YEARS LATER...

2

CHRISTMAS EVE

Only the mountain tops are white: luminous peaks in an otherwise dark landscape. The night sky is clear, the moon bright and full shining on the placid water of the lake. Another light appears in the sky that is neither a star nor the moon. The light is white and has the appearance of flames reaching down towards earth. The light precedes a ring of utter blackness, so black it makes the dark night sky look blue. The white flames appear to be pulling the ring of black towards the lake. The light is reflected in the water now and so is the circle of black. The light reaches the water and the blackness crashes into it at a speed that makes it imperceptible to the human eye. The light and the ring of blackness are now connected to the lake and although the water billows briefly it is otherwise quite calm. There is no splash, no noise, silence throughout. The only evidence of what has taken place is the perfect ring of luminous fire floating in the centre of the lake; but no one sees the evidence before it spits and dies. There is nothing left to point to what has happened: no one to witness the arrival of the Hole in Darkmere.

1 YEAR LATER…

3

*T*homas and Emily made their escape at last. They figured nobody would be working on the pontoon today of all days and they were dying to get a closer look. Neither of them could believe it when Thomas found a pair of binoculars hidden inside his mum's wardrobe ready to be wrapped, he'd never been given anything for Christmas that he'd actually asked for before. That's when they'd had the idea. Nobody would know if he just had a quick go with them and put them back after. Bill, their father snored, and their mother Dot was hypnotised by the television as they sneaked out. They knew it would be many hours before anyone would miss them so they needn't rush home. It was all going to plan. They'd waited long enough.

"Jesus. It couldn't be any colder," protested Thomas as he covered his mouth with his scarf.

It was freezing. Snow capped only the mountaintops but everywhere was white, bitten by a hard frost.

"Oh, come on!" Emily grabbed his coat and dragged him from the shelter of the porch. The wind chill was savage.

Hunched over, they trudged over the frost-hardened

ground towards the lake. They could see the tarpaulin flapping in the wind and hid behind an outcrop of rock.

"See if yer can see 'owt wi' yer bins," said Emily, blowing frosty breath into her hands.

Thomas took the shiny black binoculars out of their leather case and trained them on the tarpaulin.

"Can yer see 'owt?"

"Nope. Nothin'."

"What about at the far end of the pontoon, the bit right in't middle o't lake?"

"That's the bit I wur lookin' at. I can't see 'owt behind the tarpaulin. Whatever it is it's well wrapped up."

"Let's get closer." Emily jumped up and skidded a few metres down.

"Em wait," hissed Thomas. Emily didn't hear. "Em wait!"

Thomas got up and stumbled down after her. He called again but she still couldn't hear, the wind was carrying his voice in the wrong direction. Thomas tripped and yelled as he crashed down the hill after her.

"Thomas, what yer doin'?"

"I wur tryin' ter get yer attention. Ow! Me elbow kills. I wur tryin' ter tell yer that thur wur someone on't pontoon."

"Are yer sure?"

"Positive, 'ere take a look." Thomas handed over the binoculars.

"I 'ate ter tell yer this Thomas, but one o't lens is cracked."

"What? What am I going ter tell mum and dad?"

"Just put 'em back and don't say 'owt," she shrugged, closing one eye over the cracked lens and squinting through the other. "I can't see anyone. You sure someone wur thur?"

"Yeah, positive. He wur wearin' white."

Emily looked again. She was frowning. "How yer supposed to see someone in white against a white background?"

"It wurn't a mistake. He wur dark skinned… you know, coloured."

"Well thur's no one thur now. Come on."

"No way. I'm not goin' now. I'm telling yer thur wur someone thur."

"Yer chickenin' out."

Thomas grabbed the binoculars back and had another look. Emily was right. There was no one there. "Okay, we'll get closer and double check," he agreed.

They hid behind a windswept spruce a few metres back from the water's edge while they watched and waited.

"See, I told yer thur wur no one," Emily said adamantly.

"I don't know. I wur pretty sure."

"Come on let's go down thur. It's Christmas Eve fer goodness sake. No one works on Christmas Eve."

"Aunt Hilda's workin' in't retirement home."

"Oh, yer know what I mean."

"I'm not sure about this Em."

"I am, come on."

Emily grabbed Thomas' sleeve and darted towards a low, snow covered pile of loose rock that edged a small shingle beach. They crouched down behind the rocks. From their vantage point they could see the small jetty leading to the pontoon. The jetty was guarded with a gate. A sign said: '*Trespassers will be prosecuted.*'

"Look, the gate's locked."

"When's that ever stopped us before?"

Emily broke cover and cautiously made her way down onto the small beach near the landing stage. She sank down into the wet shingle. The wind whipped over the lake towards her. If she looked out across it she could feel the icy droplets burn her skin. She turned away and peered over the small ridge towards the jetty. She was close to the gate. Close enough to read the small print on the warning sign. The threat unnerved her, made her anxious but she didn't let on to Thomas. She knew he'd wimp out if he suspected she had the slightest doubt.

Thomas hesitated. He was sure he'd seen a man on the pontoon, but he was jumpy: the tarpaulin flapping in the wind didn't help. He could have made a mistake he supposed. Peering through his binoculars he double-checked. There was nothing. Emily was beckoning furiously. She was frowning, annoyed by his hesitation. How many times had they watched the pontoon and fantasised about what was underneath the tarpaulin? Em was convinced it had something to do with the tourists that went missing, presumed drowned, in the summer. Their bodies were never found. Shortly after the family disappeared some men wearing white overalls and masks had arrived at the lake and built the pontoon, cordoning it and a large portion of the lake off. Nobody in the village asked questions because everyone assumed the men had something to do with the police and that they were looking for the bodies of the missing family. Only later, after the pontoon and that portion of the lake were secured, did it begin to occur to Thomas and Emily that the work had nothing to do with the police.

As speculation about the purpose of pontoon began to grow, the big drill arrived. That's when Emily decided that the men were looking for oil. Thomas thought it was a sound theory but he couldn't quite put to the back of his mind concern for the missing family because it reminded him of the incident when the Garth's dog, Monty, had drowned that spring.

As if it wasn't bad enough that the Garth's dad had died, their dog had to go and drown a few months later when Thomas was supposed to have been looking after it, taking it for a walk to help the poor family out. He felt terrible about it but there was nothing he could have done. There was something about the way Monty had struggled, as though he'd been fighting against a strong current before suddenly being yanked down, as though by a shark. But Thomas knew no such current existed in the lake and there definitely weren't any sharks. His father Bill had been unsympathetic when he'd mentioned the circumstances of Monty's death, and harshly warned Thomas to keep away from the lake. The warning had done nothing but fuel his curiosity.

Since winter had set in, the men in white suits had all gone and for weeks now nobody had been seen guarding the pontoon. Thomas and Emily, isolated in Fell Side cottage by heavy snowfalls during the Christmas break, had found themselves with nothing better to do than sneak out and spy, hoping to see something of interest that might banish the boredom that always set in on winter holidays.

As Thomas looked down anxiously at his sister waiting on the tiny beach, he thought of Monty again and shuddered. After watching him drown, Thomas had lain down on that same beach where Emily was crouching now and he'd cried. Suddenly he was filled with resolve again. He needed to know what was behind that tarpaulin. It had something to do with the dog's death he was sure, and for a while now he had been coming round to Emily's original idea that it might have something to do with the missing family, he just hadn't admitted it to her.

Without further thought he broke cover and dashed across the bank. He was half way across when he heard a shout:

"Hey!"

There *was* someone there!

"Hey you!"

The call came again. It was the man in white. His dark skin was like ebony against the tarpaulin. Thomas panicked, slipped, regained his footing and sprinted back to hide behind the spruce. Panting, he turned to see if Emily was all right. She was still down on the beach cowering behind the ridge. Her eyes were wide with fear as she watched the man leap off the pontoon and run towards Thomas.

Thomas ran. He ran back up the hill where there were more trees. He could hear boots thudding towards him across the frozen landscape. They were catching him fast. Panic was welling up inside him, restricting his breath and tightening his chest, his legs were turning to jelly and he was still a long way from home yet. The man was going to catch him; he was never going to make it home before being caught.

Thomas suddenly realised he was close to the witch tree, a spiky hawthorn warped by the wind so that it looked like an angry witch. The witch tree grew against a small escarpment, and between it and the bare rock was a half decent hiding place. Thomas crouched down into the gap. He was panting wildly but silently with his hands clasped over his mouth. The heavy boots thudded past then stopped nearby. Thomas could hear the man panting. He was getting nearer. A twig snapped underfoot as he came close. Thomas wanted to scream.

"Godamnit," the man cursed. He was American. He stood close by for almost as long as Thomas could bear but then his panting became quieter. He was moving away. Thomas breathed a sigh of relief but it wasn't lasting. He had to get out, get home, sound the alarm, rescue Emily.

*

By the time Thomas reached home he was in a frenzied state. He was so badly shaken that his fingers fumbled hopelessly at the latch so that he could barely open the door. Finally he lurched into the hallway, gasping, exhausted, spent.

"Don't be so dramatic fer goodness sake," grinned Emily from the kitchen door. Her coat was off but she still had her scarf around her neck. A steaming mug of something was clasped between her hands. She sipped it.

"'Ow did yer…?"

"I took a short cut. Shush!" She nodded towards the television room looking serious all of a sudden. Thomas guessed she didn't want the olds to hear. "Get yer coat off. I'll make yer a brew," she added.

Thomas followed her into the kitchen, closing the door quietly behind him.

"What the 'ell just happened to us?"

"We wur trespassin'."

"No we wurn't. We wurn't on private land. He can't chase us like that. Who the 'ell is he any road?"

"I don't know, but if you'd seen what I'd seen you'd understand why he wur chasin' us."

"What d'yer mean? 'Yer didn't go up thur?"

"After that fella' chased yer I ran on ter pontoon."

"Yer did what? Oh Christ Em, I don't want anythin' more ter do wi' this. It feels wrong."

"It's too late. I seen what it is he's guardin' and I think he's seen me."

Thomas grabbed tufts of his hair in both hands. "What d'yer mean he's seen yer? He wur chasin me."

"I might 'ave stayed thur too long. He wur comin' back."

"Oh God, tell us it's not possible."

"What's not possible love?" Dot asked, as she strode into the kitchen and flicked the switch on the kettle to re boil it. Thomas and Emily looked at each other with startled expressions. "Making us all a brew I suppose," she mumbled in answer to her own question, then made herself a cup of tea and headed back to the television room. "Corrie Christmas special's just startin'. Not watching it loves?"

"Nah, thanks mum," they replied relieved that she hadn't quizzed them.

"D'yer think she 'eard 'owt?" said Emily, gently pushing the kitchen door too again.

Thomas was shaking his head but not in answer to her question, he was still stunned by disbelief.

"I'm tellin' yer it wur amazin'," continued Emily when she was sure her mother was out of earshot. "It wur a black Hole. It looked like it went straight down ter centre o'the earth, except I couldn't see a centre. I couldn't see 'owt, no water nothin', it wur just... well... black."

"Jesus! But 'ow can yer 'ave a Hole in't middle o't lake? 'Ow do they stop the water fillin' it up?"

"Dunno'," she shrugged, "I couldn't see 'owt holdin' it back, the water just sort o' swirled around it."

"That don't make no sense. It's too weird."

"See fer yerself. We could go back."

"No way! Yer saw that man. He didn't look like he wur out carol singin'."

Suddenly they fell quiet again. They could hear their father in the hallway. He was talking to someone at the front door. Emily lowered her voice.

"That's what makes it all't more intriguin'. I mean yer just don't go chasin' people unless yer've got summut to guard."

Thomas shuddered. He didn't want to think about it anymore. It was all too scary. "It'll be summat to do wi' money," he said dismissively. "It's always to do wi' money an' whoever's involved won't want us sticky beakin'."

"They won't know if wur careful."

"We thought we wur being careful before didn't we? No Em, I'm not goin'. I don't want anythin' more to do wi'it."

26

"Well I want to see it again otherwise I'll come ter think I wur dreamin' an' I know I wurn't. I'm goin' again tonight."

Suddenly their father yelled something and slammed the front door shut, making them both jump out of their skins. The door flew open and Bill burst into the kitchen. He was red in the face and his fists were clenched.

"What you two bin up ter?" he snarled.

"What d'yer mean dad?" replied Emily calmly. She'd always been better at handling her father than Thomas. Thomas kept his mouth shut and tried unsuccessfully to look innocent.

"I said, what yer bin up ter? Whur've yer bin all this while, while me and yer ma wur watchin' telly?"

"To our nan's dad, she asked us if we'd feed 'er chickens. She's stayin' over at Aunt Hilda's. Sharin' a glass o' sherry and stayin' over, she said, seein' as she wurn't invited 'ere." Emily could tell he believed her. He leaned into the fridge to get a can of beer.

"That woman! She bin' moanin' on again?"

"Don't matter dad. We 'ad nowt else ter do," said Thomas, feeling confident that Emily's fib had been successful.

Bill turned from the fridge and looked him straight in the eye.

"Are yer sure you bin nowhur else?"

Thomas could feel his cheeks getting hot. "Nowhur dad, honest. We just can't be doin' wi' all them soaps that's

27

all, so we thought we might as well go over ter our nan's. We watched 'er telly fer a while instead."

Emily could have punched Thomas for saying something so stupid. He always had to say too much. Now Bill only had to ask what they watched and they'd be sprung. She watched as Bill's eyes narrowed. She was screaming inside.

"Well wur not watchin' any more rubbish. I want ter catch up on events in Iraq, and I don't like yers hangin' about whisperin' in't kitchen, so ger in 'ere whur I can see yer." Bill marched out again.

Thomas and Emily breathed a huge sigh of relief.

"Who wur that at door then?" Thomas whispered worriedly, as they headed down the hall.

Emily grabbed his arm and held him back for a second.

"Never mind who wur at door, I'm goin' again Thomas. I'm goin' tonight. I'm gonna' set me alarm for one. Are you wi' me or not?"

"Not!" Thomas replied defiantly.

"Right then, I'll go on me awn." Emily picked up her drink and marched into the lounge after her father.

4

"Sit down thur whur I can keep an eye on yer, an' be quiet I want ter watch the news." Bill seized the remote control and switched the twenty-four-hour news channel on just as the true father of a young girl's baby was about to be revealed in the Coronation Street special. Dot despaired. Bill's news addiction seriously interfered with her soap watching, but she knew better than to say anything. She left the room to make another round of tea instead. Thomas stoked the dying embers of the fire and threw another log on. He wondered why it was that his dad spent most of his spare time watching the news channel these days.

Thomas broke the silence, "What's all this business in Iraq then Dad?"

"Nowt, they've found summat that's all," he grunted.

Dot returned and handed Thomas a cup of tea and a mince pie.

"Like what?" he asked, raising his eyebrows expectantly as he gingerly sipped his hot tea.

"As I said, it's nowt."

"Well it must be summat furly important if it's on't news all'time," he added with a mouthful of mince pie.

"I 'eard it wur the Holy Grail," Emily piped up.

"That Holy Grail stuff is a load o' rubbish. Thur is no Holy Grail," Thomas replied dismissively.

"Well whatever it is, they reckon half the powers of the western world want ter get thur 'ands on it. They reckon it might cause another war," added Emily.

"I suppose it could be about oil. Everyone fights over oil. It makes more sense than the flippin' Holy Grail any road. I'm beginnin' ter think you might even be right about them lookin' fer oil down by't lake Em."

Bill wheeled round angrily, "What d'yer say?" he snarled.

Thomas had said too much again. He never was any good at minding what he said. He swallowed his mouthful of mince pie dryly. "Nowt dad," he replied nervously, but Bill wasn't about to let it go.

"About lake. What wur yer sayin' 'bout it?" he growled.

"Nowt, just that they must be lookin' fer oil that's all, honest, we wur just talkin' about it that's all."

Bill rose from his chair ominously. He leaned over Thomas and repeatedly jabbed him in the chest snarling: "You keep away from that lake d'yer hear me. I won't warn yer again, yer little…" Bill decided against beating him, he would miss the rest of the news report if he did. Instead, he returned to his chair in silence. Thomas was shaken. He had a lucky escape but it didn't stop the lump rising in his throat as he fought back his tears.

After that a familiar stony silence fell over the room. Bill's volatile temper and constantly simmering annoyance meant there were many such silences in Fell Side cottage and they were often afraid.

Shush!" Bill said suddenly even though nobody had spoken.

The news programme was showing pictures of the site in Iraq that Bill was so concerned with. The site surrounded by scaffolding and tarpaulin flashed up on the screen. It was very heavily guarded. The world's press also surrounded the site but no one knew what the tarpaulin was hiding. British reporter Jack Hill was making a live report. Emily liked him so she began to pay attention.

"So what is it that the massive conglomerate Worldwide Energy Plus has found? Well no one quite knows yet. We can only imagine they must have made a significant discovery during an oil survey. The conglomerate's President, Levi Washington, has so far refused to comment. His press secretary, Ms Iman Khan, released a statement that a press conference will be called in good time but nobody knows when. In the meantime, the rest of the world is left to speculate. The most popular assumption so far is that they've discovered the actual Holy Grail. The second, and in my view more believable assumption, is that they have discovered the remains of Christ. Some senior historians, however, doubt both these theories and fear the find may be even more significant than that, if that is possible. They warn that the frenzied excitement this dig is causing should be tempered with concern. If nothing else, just look around here and see the large scale destruction that has been caused to this ancient site in search of the mystery object."

The reporter began walking around the terrible site pointing at the ancient ruins smashed by the caterpillar tracks of large vehicles, and the huge tracts of sacred earth that had been ripped up by diggers. Jack Hill was getting closer to the outer layer of security: "It will have to be an earth shattering discovery to justify this devastation," he said. "All I know is that it's something big, something the like of which has never been discovered before, something that men have been searching for since the dawn of time." Jack was about to continue when private security guards suddenly surrounded him and the cameraman and threatened them with guns. He had strayed too close.

"Did you see that?" Thomas cried, relieved to see Jack raising his hands and beating a hasty retreat.

"I did. It was weird."

"Weird, what d'yer mean weird? That fella' nearly got his head blown off. That's not weird that's horrific."

Emily lowered her voice. "I didn't mean that," she whispered. "I meant the drills, didn't yer see 'em?"

"I wur too busy lookin' at the guns aimed at that fella's head."

Emily put a finger to her lips and nodded towards the television where the news anchorwoman was apologising for the abrupt end to the live interview:

"...and we will return to that broadcast just as soon as we are able... The President of Worldwide Energy Plus, Levi Washington, has declined to comment on the desecration of archaeological sites and widespread destruction in Babylonia. Worldwide Energy Plus' press secretary Ms Iman Khan has confirmed that a statement on behalf of the conglomerate regarding their discovery will be made at nine a.m on Christmas morning."

A picture of Levi Washington flashed up on the television screen. Thomas gasped.

"What the hell's the matter wi' yer' fer god's sake?" snarled Bill.

"Me tea wur too hot dad that's all," Thomas spluttered.

"Ne'er mind yer tea bein' too hot, the back o' me 'and is gonna' make yer feel hot alright. I'm sick o' yer racket. Get outter me sight before I do yers both an injury. Gerrup them stairs and get ter bed. Go on wi' yer."

"But Dad, it's Christmas Eve. That's not fair," protested Emily.

"I don't give a monkeys, I've 'ad it wi' you two. Now ger on wi' yer, before I show yer the back o' me 'and," he raised his hand ready to carry out his threat.

Thomas and Emily scarpered up the creaky stairs.

"I didn't see the drill Em but that Levi fella, the one

that owns that big oil company, well that wur 'im what chased us down by the lake."

"I know it wur. And they wur his drills in Iraq just like the one by us lake."

"So what are they doin' by us lake?"

"I dunno' but I reckon it's summat ter do wi' that Hole."

"But what could the big deal be about a Hole?"

"I told yer Thomas. It wurn't no ordinary Hole."

5

*E*mily thought twice when the alarm went off. She pressed snooze and pulled the duvet back over her head. It was too dark, too cold and she was too tired. But then her mind began to race. She remembered the Hole, and the miles of black emptiness swirling around inside it trying to tempt her, no, drag her in. She couldn't go back to sleep now if she wanted to.

After she'd pressed snooze for the sixth time she was wide-awake. Still under the duvet, she reached one hand out and felt for her clothes on the chair. She found them, dragged them under the bedclothes, and got dressed in bed. She was still bitterly cold when she threw the covers back so she went to her chest and rooted out more socks.

It had been snowing furiously while she slept and it was already several centimetres deep on her window ledge. Her bedroom door creaked when she opened it and stepped out onto the equally creaky landing.

"Oi, whur d'yer think your goin'?"

Emily jumped out of her skin. "Yer gave us an heart attack yer idiot." Thomas was standing in his doorway. "I knew yer wouldn't be able to resist," she smiled and then looked at his pyjamas. "Get dressed then, yer can't come out dressed like that, thur's a blizzard out thur."

"I'm not comin'. It wurn't you that woke me. I 'eard voices downstairs."

"Oh, what are they still doin' up?" Emily sighed impatiently.

"I can hear dad but mum's asleep in her room I checked. It's a woman's voice though and sometimes they sound like thur arguin'."

Then Emily heard it too, raised voices coming from the lounge. Thomas was right, one of them was female and it wasn't her mum. Emily sneaked across the landing to see if she could hear more. The woman shouted again. Fearful, Emily crept back to Thomas' doorway.

"D'yer reckon' he's havin' an affair?" Thomas whispered worriedly.

"What, our dad!"

"Well, why else would 'e let some woman boss 'im 'round?"

Emily was afraid. She remembered her dad arguing with someone at the front door earlier, but she hadn't bothered enquiring about it because she had been too wrapped up in her own story. Now she was wondering if the two visits were connected and if so were they something to do with the Hole? But that was too far fetched, Emily told herself. Apart from the man, there hadn't been anyone else on the pontoon and it was definitely a woman's voice down stairs, not a man, and definitely not an American. No, Thomas was right, their father was having an affair. It was a much less terrifying explanation.

The living room door suddenly opened out onto the hallway.

"Oh, cripes hide!" Thomas ran back into his room and dived under his duvet. Emily couldn't get back to her room without being seen on the landing, so she dived behind Thomas' door, spying through a gap by the hinge. They were climbing the stairs. The woman emerged into the dim light, followed closely by Bill.

"Are you sure she will not wake?" they heard the woman ask. Her accent was rich and exotic. Emily could just about make her out. She was slender and dark, taller than Bill, even without her heels.

"Sure. I gave 'er one o't pain killers I use fer't cattle. I mixed it in 'er 'ot chocolate."

Emily couldn't believe it. He'd drugged her mother so that he could carry on right under her nose, in her own house. She wanted to leap out, surprise them, shame them; but something stopped her, something about the woman terrified her. Then Emily froze. The woman was going into her room. Emily's door creaked open.

"Where is the girl?" the woman snarled angrily.

Bill was perplexed. "What d'yer mean? I sent 'er to bed hours ago."

The woman's face clouded with anger. "The boy? In which room does he bed?"

"Yer said yersel' the boy saw nowt."

"She will have told him by now. They were in it together."

"Come on, leave 'im be."

"Mr Hayward you know what the alternative is. If I have to send Mr Washington…"

"Alright, alright. His room's over 'ere."

Emily watched her father approach Thomas' bed but she couldn't see the woman, she hadn't come far enough into the room.

"Thomas lad, wake up. Thomas, Thomas." Bill shook his son and gradually pulled the duvet from his face. Emily could tell even in the dim light that he was pretending to be asleep, his body was too rigid and his eyes too squashed shut. But Bill didn't seem to notice. "Thomas lad, come on gerrup now, there's a boy." He began lifting Thomas' shoulders from the bed, trying to sit him. Thomas could pretend no more. He was petrified.

"Eh, what is it?" he asked, blinking as though he'd just woken.

"I need yer ter get dressed lad. I need yer ter do it quickly."

"Ask him where the girl is." The woman's voice was sharp and cold.

Emily shivered behind the door, cold and terrified all at once.

"What's goin' on dad? Who's she?" Thomas' voice trembled.

"No one yer need ter worry about son."

But Thomas was worried. His father didn't talk to him so softly normally. It was as though he was being apologetic.

"The girl!" The woman's icy tones chilled the room again.

"Whur's our Em Thomas? Some folk need ter speak ter 'er."

"What sort o' folk?" Thomas asked, staring at the woman and not daring to look at his sister's shadowy figure crouching behind the door.

"Important people."

"What do they want ter know 'bout dad? Our Em dun't know owt' about owt'. Yer know that, yer always sayin' she'll never pass 'er exams the way she carries on."

"Can't you get on with it fool?" the woman hissed.

"Look son, ne'er mind all that," Bill continued as softly as he was able. His huge gnarled and dirty hands were oppressive on Thomas' shoulders. "We just need ter find our lass that's all. She could be in grave danger if we don't find 'er."

Thomas squinted. Now he was unsure. Perhaps they were here to protect Emily and get her before someone else did. That would make sense, he thought. That's why their dad was involved, this woman had come to protect them.

But Emily was shaking her head vigorously from behind the door, apparently not as convinced.

"She's gone down tu't lake," Thomas said nervously looking from one to the other of them. The woman stared at him. She was suspicious.

"Why that little…" Bill snarled angrily.

"Like a moth to a light bulb." The woman smiled. "Well we had better go and get her then, before someone else finds her first. Bring the boy," she added sternly.

Bill grabbed Thomas' arm but Thomas resisted.

"Whur yer takin' us? I'm knackered and cold dad. I just want ter go ter bed."

"Yer can't son. Yer must come wi' me." Bill pulled Thomas past the woman and out of the room. They stopped on the landing and turned when they realised the woman had not followed. Thomas' heart was in his mouth. She was searching the room. She hadn't been fooled. She looked straight at him. She smiled. Thomas knew his look of horror was a give away but it had been too late to hide it. She'd seen it.

"Ah, come on, the lad doesn't lie." Bill said impatiently.

The woman stopped in the doorway and narrowed her eyes as she stared at Thomas. "Everybody lies," she said coldly, before closing the bedroom door behind her.

6

*E*mily was still crouching in the shadow behind Thomas' bedroom door when she heard the front door slam shut. There was silence but for her quick breathing and the thumping of her heart, like a fist on a drum; she wondered that it had not given her away it seemed so loud.

She remained huddled in the darkness for some time after the woman and Bill had left with Thomas. She imagined a terrified Thomas being frogmarched across the ice and snow in little more than his pyjamas. If he didn't freeze to death they were going to kill him, she was sure of that. That meant she had to do something; but what? A dark image of the Hole flashed across her mind. Her curiosity had been excited by it when she'd stood before it yesterday, watching with amazement the tonnes of lake water just slapping around the smooth sides of black emptiness. *How did it do that*? She hadn't understood then the full measure of danger surrounding the Hole. The darkness deep inside it had almost hypnotised her and she'd swayed almost falling in, almost wanting to fall in.

Now though she felt the weight of the trouble it had

brought: real trouble, serious trouble; the sort of trouble that would turn a father against his own son, against his whole family. Emily shuddered. It was all so deadly serious. She had to escape. She had to get help.

Even though Emily was sure the woman and her father had gone she was still afraid of being caught, so she crept cautiously out onto the landing. Her mother's bedroom door was open. Emily peered in. The room was eerily quiet, but she knew the disquietingly still mound under the duvet was her mother's body. Emily tiptoed towards the bed and swept back the duvet. A wave of relief washed over her as she watched the steady rise and fall of her mother's chest, indicating that she was not dead. The drugs had put her in a deep sleep, her complexion looked drained and not a muscle twitched but at least she was not dead.

Emily placed a hand on her mother's shoulder and gently shook her. Dot was unresponsive. Emily shook her harder until Dot's body rolled over but she still did not wake. Disappointed, Emily replaced the duvet and reached for the bedside telephone. She dialled, 9...9...9... and waited for the voice on the other end to tell her what to do. No voice came. It wasn't even ringing. Emily pressed the handset to her other ear as though it would make a difference but there wasn't even a dialling tone: the line was dead. Emily threw the telephone across the room in frustration and buried her face in her hands.

A sudden, terrifying realisation made tears come thick

and fast: if the phone lines were down her only hope was to beat a path through the ice and snow to get to the village on the other side of Scar Fell. In this weather, the village may as well have been on another planet.

Emily zipped up and slammed the cottage door shut behind her. The bitter wind scorched her face and ears, so she pulled her scarf up to cover them. Darkmere village was at least two miles away from Fell Side cottage. The roads were probably thick with snow by now because it hadn't stopped snowing for hours. Emily trudged on regardless, trying not to feel beaten by the freezing wind that was trying to erode her determination with its relentlessness.

Eventually she arrived at the place where the road should be. On an ordinary day the road would have taken her all the way around the base of Scar Fell and into the village on the other side. Now the road had been completely whitewashed by a perfect layer of deep snow.

With thoughts of Thomas and her mother at the forefront of her mind, she determined to follow the road round despite the snow. Less than five minutes later, however, she'd stopped and was doubled over, digging her fingers into the burning stitch in her ribs and gasping for breath. The snow was too deep. She was sinking to her knees with every step. It made each step exhausting and time consuming. Emily straightened up again and pulled the scarf back over her face. As she looked out over the deep uniform layer of snow that buried the road ahead, she thought of Frank Garth the postman.

It was only last Christmas when he'd been heading home from a party on a similar snowy night. Unable to pass the mounting snow covered roads in his car, Frank had decided to walk the last few hundred yards to the warmth of his cottage. They'd found him the next morning frozen and dead. His wife hadn't been able to sound the alarm when he did not return as the phone lines were down, and nobody could have got to him in time even if she had.

It wasn't really the shock of Frank's death that affected her, as much as her sudden understanding of the savagery of the elements. Snow had always been something she'd prayed for, the deeper the better. She'd never considered for a second that it could be dangerous, that it could kill. Since the news of Frank's death though, she viewed winter with suspicion, and a falling of deep snow did not fill her with joyful abandon as it had done before.

The recollection of Frank's death made Emily realise that her intention to get to the village by means of the road was sheer folly. It wasn't going to happen. She would die, and if she died who would help her mother and Thomas before it was too late? Emily looked up at Scar Fell's menacing north face. The snow, made luminous everywhere else by the bright moonlight, remained in dark shadow on its steep, craggy, north side. It was as though the darkness served as a warning to her.

"I'm never gonna make it up there," she said to herself. Tears formed and began streaming down her face, soaking her scarf until it became cold against her face. She felt insignificant, like a dot in the sprawling white landscape and as vulnerable to the wild elements as a newborn baby in a lion's den.

Still gasping for breath and still trying to squeeze the stitch out of her side, Emily studied Scar Fell's black face more closely. The enormity and solidity of it made her wince but she'd climbed it before. She'd climbed it with Thomas. It had been a clear day with the summer sun on their backs but at least she knew she could do it. Emily began to feel more positive suddenly. She looked up and could just about make out the small rocky outcrop near the summit: a natural platform known as the 'pulpit' upon which climbers could rest and survey the land beyond the mountain they had conquered. It was lit by the moon like a star on top of a Christmas tree and like a beacon of hope, or a portent of doom – she didn't know which – it beckoned her towards it.

The north side of the mountain was at least sheltered from the bitter wind and Emily felt comparatively warm within its embrace. It also meant there was less snow cladding it. In places bare rock was visible so that she could make out some of the crag's great boulders around the base of Scar Fell. Being able to see them made them seem easier to navigate than the featureless snow bound road. It was the deep crevasses between the boulders that she needed to avoid. In the wintry darkness, it seemed like the crag belonged to an entirely different world, one where creatures could be hiding in the crevasses, waiting to grab your ankles and drag you into their dark underworld forever. Every nerve and fibre of Emily as she clambered over the crag was tense and on high alert for fear of falling or slipping into a rock coffin. But she hadn't fallen or slipped and now she was off the crag and standing beneath the waterfall. On any other night the waterfall would be plunging over the escarpment, but on this night it was eerily still, frozen, as though in time.

Emily took a moment to catch her breath and give her nerves time to stop trembling. She would follow Scar Fell gill up the mid section of the mountain until she reached Lord's Rake, but then what? How would she get up the almost vertical rake alive in this weather? She could see its long sheer passage, deep and black like a wound, as though it was the result of some act of savage violence: a slash down the mountain's face, the reason for its name. Emily began to tremble again. Thinking about the rake before she had to would get her nowhere and she feared she might talk herself out of going any further. So she buried the terrifying thought of its almost impossible passage; besides, despite everything, it just didn't feel like the night she would die.

Grabbing the wintry branches of well-rooted shrubs, Emily managed to scramble up the relatively gentle incline of Scar Fell's mid section with something approaching ease. She cut herself only once when she slipped on a sharp exposed rock but otherwise the ascent was going well, that is until it started to snow again. Large flakes began sticking to her frozen face and eyelashes. Emily had long since stopped being able to feel her hands. Numb hands made gripping the shrubs and scrambling over cold wet rocks increasingly difficult. Soaking wet and perilously cold, she was tiring and that meant she was slipping with increasing frequency. Eventually, she persuaded herself to stop and rest, not realising straightaway that she was already standing below Lord's Rake, and that its dark scar was pointing straight down at her.

Despite glistening in the moonlight, the treacherous ice clad scar looked darker and more menacing than ever. Emily quailed; her nerve faltered and she felt the night might have death in it after all. She took a moment to think about the possibility that her life might end soon, in the next few hours or minutes… by morning she might be no more.

Her eyes welled up but she was calm. She would prefer to die trying to save her mother and brother than live knowing she had not tried. Understanding that gave Emily strength. In the end she would prefer to give herself up to the 'Grim Reaper', as the rake was locally known, than live forever with guilt. Emily looked up at the rake once more. As she took in the details of its jagged edges and steep almost vertical passage, clad in ice, she prayed that the Grim Reaper had chosen this night to be abroad.

*

It seemed Emily only remembered to breathe when she finally climbed into the pulpit at the top of the rake. Adrenalin, fear, drive, a combination of all those things had caused her to blank out the pain and the cold, enabling her to push on up to the top in an almost hypnotic state. When she reached the pulpit and clambered into its relatively safe embrace, she wasn't entirely aware of how she'd got there. Her knees shook so badly she couldn't understand how she was still managing to stand. Then she did stop standing and collapsed down onto her knees. Her hands burned and throbbed and she held them in front of her trying to work out if they were burning because they were bleeding, or cold, or both, but she couldn't tell. Looking at them though made her remember how they came to be bleeding in the first place. It was also how her coat came to be ripped and her chin split open. She placed a trembling hand underneath her jaw and touched the gash, gasping from the raw pain she felt.

Lumps of clotted blood that had formed in her mouth made her retch and she spat the dark lumps out onto the bright ice. How far had she fallen, she wondered? It hadn't been all the way down, that would have killed her, but she'd fallen far enough, landing on a small fragile ledge, the edge of which was crumbling and threatening to collapse with every muscle she moved. She hadn't even so much fallen as slid down the rake, catching her chest and her chin on exposed outcrops of rock, frantically clawing with her fingernails to stop her fall from gathering pace.

It felt as though she'd fallen for miles. Every fraction of a second seemed like an hour, such was the acuteness of her pain; and then, just when she thought she was never going to stop and this was her end, she did stop on the small fragile ledge. Still in her hypnotic state somehow from somewhere she'd found the strength and courage to go on, to get back on her feet and climb again. It wasn't as though she'd had any choice, and now she was standing in the pulpit at the top: a challenge met, a fear conquered, help one step nearer. Hope was in sight.

The descent was bliss by comparison. The gently rolling slope of Scar Fell's south side was more of a tricky winter ramble than a climb. In clement weather you needed little more than a pair of sturdy walking boots to meet the challenges of its friendlier side. The south side was, however, covered in deep snow and the sharp, cruel, north wind battered her unhindered. Emily was undeterred though, spurred on by a temporary sense of infallibility after climbing the rake, and by the sight of a sprinkling of lights from the village below. There were not as many lights as usual she noticed but she guessed a lot of power was down.

As she neared the village, Emily began to worry about what she would say to the police when she got there. How could she explain herself so that they would take her seriously and act quickly? What if they told her to wait until first light? She'd heard that expression before on the news. She hoped she would not hear them use it tonight, 'first light' would equal too late.

Suddenly Emily's leg buckled beneath her. She tripped and fell, rolling and rolling. First snow in her face, then air, then snow, then air, snow, air, snow, snow, snow; mouthfuls of it. She was confused when she came to a halt. Her coat had become entangled in a barbed wire fence that had caught her like a net. Bits of naked skin on her face, neck and wrists were hooked and bleeding. She felt like lying there and crying indefinitely. With painful fingers, however, she unhooked her clothes and her skin and stumbled towards a nearby stile. She wasn't about to give up now. Emily climbed the style and pressed on. It stopped snowing and the wind dropped a little. How mild it felt, she thought, once the wind dropped and the icy snow had stopped sticking to her. Before she knew it she was stumbling through Darkmere village.

At last Emily stood trembling before the big blue door of the police station. The door symbolised all hope. Emily banged on it with as much force as she could muster. There was no answer. It hadn't occurred to her that it might not be manned on Christmas day. She had known such an instance before when all calls were referred to the big station in Windermere, a further six miles away by snow bound road.

Panicking slightly, Emily turned and looked at the other dwellings with lights on. Did she know any of them, she wondered? Yes, Sharon Huddleston, the post-mistress' daughter: number two, Tarnside Lane. Emily was about to turn and head for the row of terraced houses where Sharon lived when the door of the police station opened.

7

"*R*uddy 'ell lass! Look at state o' yer. What in God's name brings y'ere on a night like this?"

PC Birkett filled the whole doorway. He looked like a God she thought, with the light from the police station framing his solid, heroic body. It was the best welcome she'd ever had from anyone, anywhere, ever. Her relief was so great upon seeing the policeman that she fell to her knees, as though finally her exhaustion had caught up with her and overwhelmed her. PC Birkett gently scooped her up and carried her into the warmth of the station. Emily was suddenly unable to control her tears.

"It's our..." she gulped, "it's our..." but she couldn't get the words out.

PC Birkett sat her down on the comfiest chair he could find. "Say no more lassy. Lerrus get yer warmed up good and proper. How about a nice hot brew? Tea alright?"

Guiding the gas fire in her direction, he turned it up full pelt and took a blanket from the only cell that was there. Emily continued to cry unabated while he helped her out of her soaking coat and wrapped her up in the blanket. The

51

kettle had finished boiling by the time her sobbing began to wane and by the time he handed her a steaming mug of tea she felt ready to talk.

"…it wur an 'Ole like I've never seen before. It wur weird 'ow the water from the lake just held itself back, as though thur wur an invisible wall holdin' it all back. Our Thomas and me reckon it's got summat to do wi' those tourists that went missin', an' Thomas said the way the Garth's dog drowned wur unnatural an' all, as though it wur pulled in t'ut lake by a strong tide or summat, but everyone knows thur in't no tide in Darkmere, and then that man chased our Thomas, yer knaw that coloured one from the telly, the one to do wi' all that stuff in Iraq, and the next thing I know is they're lookin' fer me, and they've taken our Thomas an…"

"Whey! Slow down lassy. Take another sip of yer tea."

Emily was panting, reliving the story made the adrenalin pump through her veins again.

PC Birkett was frowning. He wasn't used to taking kids seriously, they had such over active imaginations, but she had been driven against all nature to get help in such terrible conditions, that it was a miracle she was not dead. That meant something bad of some description must have happened. Something terrible had driven her here on a night like this. She was so distraught, however that he suspected her story was probably wildly inaccurate, especially trying to link the missing tourists and the dead dog with a Hole in the middle of Darkmere: all that was pure fantasy.

"Whur wur Bill while all this wur goin' on?" he asked frowning.

"Oh, he's one of 'em. He was wi' 'er, yer knaw, the woman, and together they took our Thomas," her eyes were wide and round, she looked wild and desperate as she nodded furiously in an effort to persuade him that her story was true.

Now PC Birkett was feeling decidedly unsure about her. He'd known Bill since they were at school together and although he was well aware of Bill's temper, he struggled to believe he could be involved in anything of the nature she was describing. Kidnapping his own son just didn't square with the man he knew.

Emily sensed he was unsure. His response was too slow. It seemed he had more concern for her than for them. She hadn't explained herself well enough: he didn't believe her. He probably thought they'd gone looking for a lost sheep together, a common enough problem on such winter nights, and she'd turned it into something else with her over active imagination. That's what grown ups put everything down to, an over active imagination, she was sure it was what PC Birkett was thinking.

"Are yer sure they didn't go lookin' fer lost sheep to rescue? It's that sort o' night."

I knew it, she thought, although she said nothing. She didn't trust herself to say the right thing, she just clenched her jaw instead. She wished she'd kept the bit about her dad to herself. Now he was gonna' say that first light thing she could tell, because he didn't believe her.

He didn't say it though, he could see the state she was in, her bleeding hands, gashed chin and ripped coat, not to mention her hard stare: measures of her determination, a determination born from some terrible fear no matter how ridiculous it sounded to him. PC Birkett was concerned enough to put on his coat and investigate matters for himself.

"You wait 'ere while I bring landrover round t'front. Then I'll tekk yer 'ome an' see fer mesell what's goin' on up at Fell Side Cottage."

"The roads are blocked. Yer couldn't get a snow plough through 'em," she said in a perplexed manner.

"How in the 'ell did you get 'ere then?" he gasped in astonishment.

"I came o'er Scar Fell."

"*Yer did what*?"

"It wur the only way fer us to get help. The phone lines are down and the road is blocked."

"Ruddy 'ell lass, yer must be crazier than a border collie wi' sunstroke. By eck! I just can't believe it... o'er Scar Fell on a night like this... an' the rake an' all, an' yer still alive!" PC Birkett paced around the station clutching his forehead and looking at her as though she was a phantom. "No wonder's yers in such a state." Then he fell silent, as though he was thinking. "Well yer might as well mekk yersell at 'ome 'ere lassy. The TV's over thur and, well yer saw wur t'kettle wur." He was buttoning up his thick coat.

Emily's heart was racing. Was he really saying what she thought he was saying?

He could read the question in her face and answered it: "I can't tekk yer wi' me lass. It would be right irresponsible. It's a wonder yer made it 'ere alive in't first place but now yer 'ere it's my responsibility to keep yer safe. Look at yer, yer exhausted. I'll go on me own and see fer mesell if Thomas is alright."

"Yer can't leave us, I'll go mad wi' worry..." she protested.

But PC Birkett ignored her and began writing something down on a piece of paper. "WPC Turner is due to tekk over in't mornin'," he said. "If I'm not back be then she can raise the alarm. I'll leave this note 'ere for 'er explainin' what's goin' on and you can get yersell some sleep. Hey! What the..."

Emily dashed for the door. She wasn't going to be stuck in a police station all night, driven mad by helplessness. No! She would rather die. She had to do something. She slid the first two bolts back easily but she couldn't release the catch on the main lock, not before she felt a big hand on her arm.

"Come on lass," he said gently, "I know it'll be tough. Don't mekk us handcuff yer so's all youse got to think on are yer troubles and worries fer't rest o't night. I don't want it ter come ter that. As I say, put yer feet up, mekk a brew, watch a bit of Christmas telly."

Emily quickly realised that escape would almost certainly be futile if she was handcuffed as well, so she acquiesced and he let her go.

PC Birkett turned to face her from the open door. "Right lass. You remember ter get yersell some rest. Don't yer be worryin' about that brother o' yours. I'll see to it he'll come to no 'arm, okay." He was just about to turn and leave when he added: "Promise me yer'll get some rest won't yer?"

Emily could tell by the worry on his face that he was hesitating, summoning up the courage to go outside and face Scar Fell in the terrible weather. He had not bargained on the night turning out this way and she felt bad for him, responsible for putting him at risk, as though everything were entirely her fault. Emily nodded to reassure him that she would indeed get some rest and be okay.

PC Birkett nodded back. "Oh well, I'll see yer later no doubt," he said not sounding as though he really believed his own words. Then he stepped outside and locked the door behind him.

As soon as the station door was closed, Emily was up looking for a means of escape. She tried the main door briefly but knew that would be pointless: a police station's front door was going to be about the most secure in existence. She was right and gave up quickly before investigating the windows. Most of the windows were barred or made of glass reinforced by steel wire: all except one. Above the desk where the note to WPC Turner lay was a small window. Emily climbed onto a chair and pushed all the files on the window ledge to the floor. She tried the handle but it was locked firmly. She needed a key. There was one on a hook right in the corner next to the window. How ridiculous she thought, to lock a window and then hang the key on a hook right next to it, especially in a police station of all places. The key slid in and Emily lifted the handle pushing the window open. A cold blast of air took her breath away again, bitterly reminding her of the journey ahead. It was so dangerous out there. She recoiled from it, allowing herself a moment to think.

Just as she was about to squeeze through the open window, she thought about the note to WPC Turner. She couldn't resist taking a look so she climbed back down and slid it round on the table to face her.

Dear WPC Turner.

Have gone down to Fell Side Cottage to investigate the disappearance of Thomas Hayward. His sister Emily reported him missing. I suspect the lad's gone looking for lost sheep with his father but the lass says it's got something to do with some adventure down at the lake getting out of hand. Any road the lass is in a bit of a state so I thought I'd better go and check out her story. If I'm not back by first light

sound the alarm, if I am then you won't be reading this letter
because I'll be telling you all about the trouble they're both
in meself,
Derek.

She knew he hadn't taken her seriously. He hadn't even mentioned the Hole or the missing tourists. If Thomas turns up dead in the morning everyone's just gonna' think he's drowned like the tourists and the dog, and not been murdered at all. 'What was wrong with old folk?' Emily thought. 'They always thought 'owt to do with kids was summat about nothing.' Emily wrote a second note:

WPC Turner,
Our Thomas has been kidnapped by some evil woman.
Levi Washington, the man on the telly who owns that big oil
company, chased our Thomas yesterday and I think he's got
something to do with it all and there's a huge black Hole that
they're guarding down there. It's all got something to do with
those missing tourists and the Garth's dog that drowned. It's
no ordinary Hole. Send lots of help. This is big!!!!!!
Emily Hayward

She underlined the word big several times and added six exclamation marks. WPC Turner would have to check it out now. Satisfied with her letter at least, Emily squeezed through the small window and was free.

8

*E*mily was in terrible pain when she came to a halt with a whack against a boulder. She rested up against it, waiting for her nerves to stop jangling and her muscles to stop twitching from the pain of a deep wound in her leg. She'd acquired it on the heady descent of Scar Fell's rake. Shivering, she watched PC Birkett below her clambering clumsily over the crag. Despite the gash in her leg, descending Scar Fell's north side had definitely been easier than ascending it she decided, as she squeezed the gash in her leg as though she could stick the torn sides of skin back together.

Emily continued to watch PC Birkett battle his way through the drifts that would take him over the hill and out of sight. When she reached the hump of the hill she could see him again. He hadn't progressed very far at all, his black figure distinct against the white snow. Whether by coincidence or not, he turned as though he had seen her. Instinctively she threw herself to the ground and only when she was lying in the cold wet snow did she wonder why she was hiding from him, it wasn't as though he could send her back now.

From her vantage point she could see that PC Birkett was looking all around him in a puzzled manner. Every time he was about to set off again he stopped doubled back and began looking about again. His strange behaviour made her curious enough to decide that it was time to catch him up and see for herself what it was he was looking for.

"Yer must be made o'ghost flesh. Thur can be no other explanation fer it," he said as she approached, battle weary but pleased with herself considering the circumstances.

"Yer knew I couldn't wait. It'd kill me ter wait."

"I didn't know such a thing and if I 'ad knawn I woulda' thrown yer in a cell wi' nowt more than some 'ot liquid fer company."

"I would've escaped that an' all, so it wurn't worth yer while tryin'"

"Aye, no doubt yer right. Yer made o' some right funny stuff yer are. I never met another'un like yer."

"Aye, so don't bother tryin' ter keep us out o' this murderous business. Yer can't, they want me I told yer. They want me as much as our lad an' I can't be kept safe from 'em even if yer lock us up."

"Now then lassy, don't be getting' all daft about that business down by t'lake again or..." PC Birkett paused, "thur it goes again."

"What, what is it?"

"I keep 'earin' a groanin' noise, like some wretched tortured soul. I think it's comin' from that gorse o'er thur."

60

Emily heard it too and it made her stomach churn with anxiety. The noise frightened her, it sounded almost human and she thought of Thomas, and she thought of him injured and hurt.

"Stand back while I tekk a look," said PC Birkett pushing past her. But Emily did not stand back. She shadowed PC Birkett as he edged forward towards the thick spiky gorse. What could be in there, in that mass of dense thorns, what state would human flesh be in if it got entangled in those thorns, she wondered? Some of the branches were moving. Something was in there: something was dying in there.

"Be careful," she whispered over PC Birkett's shoulder.

PC Birkett jumped. "Blimey lass, I thought I told yer ter stand back. Don't yer ever do 'owt yer told?"

Emily shrugged and then a groan and a crunching of snow made her start. PC Birkett shoved Emily backwards then he leapt forward, and using his coat for protection from the spiky branches he parted them.

"Argh!" he cried out, falling forwards as though he'd been dragged into the bushes.

"PC Birkett!"

He was back on his feet now and even in the darkness Emily could see that his face was stained with blood. He was staring into the gorse as though he couldn't believe what he was seeing.

"PC Birkett?" she said again unable to find the words to say more.

"It's alright lass. It's alright," he said at length, but his voice was tremulous and as he wiped his face, she could see that his hands were trembling too. He was afraid. Emily had never seen a grown man as afraid as he looked now.

"What wur it? Yer covered in blood?" she quizzed.

"Am I?" He seemed surprised when he wiped his cheek again and saw the blood on his hand as a result. Then he shuddered. "Ne'er mind. I'm alright, that's the main thing."

"But what wur it? What could be alive in thur?"

"It wur a sheep that's all. It looks as though it's been stranded fer some time. Broken a leg most likely, then stumbled inter't gorse and got stuck. It's out of its misery now."

Emily was suspicious. He wasn't telling her the truth about what was in the gorse. He was too afraid for it to have been a dead sheep.

"Can I see," she tried to peer past him but he held her firmly.

"It's not a pretty sight."

"Nowt I 'aven't seen before," she protested trying to get past him.

"Give it up I'm tellin' yer," PC Birkett grabbed her arms and was suddenly angry.

"But yer wur dragged in ter't bushes," she protested. Then she stopped, she could see it was wrong to press him. There was something wrong. Something he was not telling her. What if it was Thomas dying, she panicked.

"Now thur yer go again lass. I wurn't dragged in no wur, I tripped an' fell an' got scratched by the gorse. It's not very excitin' but thur it is. That's all thur is to it. Ye'll drive yersell mad wi' that imagination o'yers one day. Now let's just get to that cottage and gerruselves a brew. I'm feelin' right short o' temper I am, an' I really don't like the way this night is turnin' out," and with that he marched off towards the cottage.

9

*I*t was cold outside. The snow swirled incessantly. The wind carried clouds of it into drifts and the ground was obscured with a cold white blanket. Darkness had fallen. Jeremiah snuggled under his duvet watching the silent flakes dissolve on the windowpane. He shivered but he was not cold: he was wondering how he'd got there.

Beyond the window he could see lights pinging out all over the castle. It must be late, he thought. The lights going out made it even darker outside, gloomier in fact. He wondered anxiously when his light would go out and he pulled the duvet around him more tightly. The lights made him think of Shae-nae. He wondered if she was behind one of them. He hoped she was. It made her feel close if he thought that. He remembered their first meeting. It was strange, like a dream and he had not liked her; but he wished she were with him now, it would be better than being alone. Now they were lost, apart from each other in this godforsaken castle, like characters in a horror movie.

There was a knock on his door. He didn't answer. The door opened anyway as he knew it would. It was the sprite again. Jeremiah looked out of the window. He couldn't look at its slimy grey skin without feeling sick. The sprite didn't make a sound as it slid across the room and placed a tray of piping hot food on the table before leaving. The food smelled good. It was hard to resist. Throwing back the covers Jeremiah climbed out of bed and sneaked, even though he was alone, across the room to the table. It was soup and bread. The bread was plain. He wolfed it while eyeing the soup suspiciously. The soup looked horrible but smelled good. His stomach rumbled. Jeremiah obeyed his instincts and ate.

When he woke he was lying on the floor beneath the table. It was dark and only the moonlight gave some vague form to the room. He'd been drugged again. He felt like he'd slept for an eternity and wasn't even sure if it was the same night. A fire ignited in the grate. He realised he was cold so he crawled over to it. Though nothing surprised him any more he thought it odd that a steaming hot milk drink should be waiting for him by the hearth. He drank it. It was bitter. He began to shiver. He could feel himself sliding into sleep again.

*

Shae-nae leapt behind the door as soon as she heard the lock click. It wasn't easy. Her head still ached terribly. She couldn't remember why. The rangy grey creature slid in and scanned the room briefly. She could not tell if it was concerned or otherwise when it failed to spot her. Its skin was repulsive. She didn't want to go near it but she was fired up... desperate... and from behind its neck looked weak. Shae-nae leapt out. She was quick. The sprite struggled but her grip was strong. It began to make a choking sound as she squeezed harder, its skinny neck squelching beneath her fingers like wet dough. Then slipping from her grip like a ripe banana, the sprite reformed itself, unharmed, by the table. Shae-nae watched suspiciously as it placed the food down. She ignored the rumbling in her belly; she would die rather than eat it. Then it left. It didn't look at her. Her threatening expression was wasted.

Apart from the food there was nothing else of any note on the table or in the room. She'd searched it a dozen times since they'd locked her in. How many times had she seen that bedpan under the bed and hoped it was a clue, a solution, but it wasn't. It was just a bedpan: the same bedpan. She dragged it out any way and double-checked. As she'd expected it was empty. She slumped on the floor and wondered where Jeremiah was. Did she even care? She'd never met an American before and she decided she didn't like them. He'd looked down his nose at her. She was used to that, but somehow it hurt more in this desperate place. Shae-nae stared at the endless turrets outside and wondered which light he was behind, if any. She crushed a fleeting feeling of hopelessness. Even if she could get out where would she go? Where was she? She stopped herself thinking. First she must get out, she would worry about the rest later.

The sprite entered the room again. She examined its movements carefully even though it was difficult to look at. It wasn't just its disgusting skin that made it repulsive, somehow it kept reminding her of stuff about herself she wanted to forget. She shuddered again as she watched it take the untouched tray and leave.

After the sprite closed the door Shae-nae crossed the room to the table and looked at the spot where the tray had rested. There was nothing there, no clue, nothing. She was used to finding solutions and finding them quickly. She was used to living off her wits, that's how she survived. She'd been locked up for days without being able to do a thing. This was not the way things usually turned out for her. Shae-nae became suddenly angry. She kicked the table hard. The table leg sheared off and slid towards the wall. Shae-nae picked the leg up. It was weighty. It was blunt. It would require both hands and a good swing but she had her solution.

The sprite was due again soon. Shae-nae waited behind the door. The lock rattled, the door opened and the sprite entered. Shae-nae lifted the table leg, it was heavy and it squelched down through the creature's head with ease. The sprite stumbled momentarily, but somehow its head reformed and it continued towards the broken table unharmed. Shae-nae wasn't about to give up. She followed it and swung the table leg again, this time like a baseball bat, right through its spindly neck. The sprite's neck stretched and almost came apart but, like elastic, it sprang back again. It stumbled though, and almost dropped the tray. 'This is it,' thought Shae-nae, 'this is my only chance.' She swung again quicker, harder. This time the head was severed. The tray dropped to the floor with a terrible clatter. The creature did not get up. It lay still on the floor, head and body separate. Shae-nae felt weak and sick, as though she herself had been beaten. She almost couldn't find the strength to move, but the door was open.

*

Jeremiah couldn't remember getting back into bed. He was still aching all down his left side. Shooting pains shot through his shoulder and reverberated around the left side of his head but he couldn't remember why he should be in such pain. All he could remember was that he'd spent a lot of time in bed since he'd arrived in the castle. He felt hopeless, depressed: nobody had even spoken to him, nobody told him why. He stared out of the window again. It was all he could think of doing. It was still dark and still snowing. He couldn't remember seeing any daylight. He bit his lip and felt a lump rising in his throat. He wouldn't have even been at home that day looking at the stupid light on the driveway if he hadn't got himself suspended from school for hacking into their computer system, he would have been abroad on a skiing trip with his other classmates. Jeremiah groaned; all he remembered, apart from his father's fury, was that he'd woken staring at the light. Ultimately, it seemed as though it had led him to this place but he couldn't remember how. Sitting up on the edge of the bed, Jeremiah decided there had to be a way out. He looked out of the window but the drop looked infinite. There had to be another way. The sprite came in again and glided across the room. It took his half eaten meal and left. The sprite had to be the way out.

Jeremiah waited patiently for the sprite to return. The door clicked. He could feel his heart thudding furiously as it entered. He could barely look at it but he would have to touch it. He would have to kill it. Jeremiah leapt on the creatures back. The floor came at him. He landed with a thud and lay winded, watching the creature reform itself by the table before placing a new meal upon it. The sprite left. Jeremiah curled up in a ball. Nobody could hear him crying.

*

Shae-nae looked both ways down the corridor. Either way was endless. She felt as though she was looking down a tube. Her heart skipped a beat and her resolve faltered like a dying bulb. She readjusted mentally. It was unrealistic to expect things to get easier at this stage, she told herself, but at least she was out, she had to stay strong. Both ways were exactly the same. She didn't know what was at the end of either, so it didn't matter which way she went. Her instincts made her take a right. She ran, where to, she wasn't sure. Perhaps she should try to find Jeremiah. She didn't like him but they were in the same boat. They both needed to escape.

*

The door clicked. Jeremiah was hiding behind the door again. He could feel his heart thudding furiously as the sprite entered the room. He leapt on the creatures back again and jammed the bedpan over its head. The creature was confused, its arms flailing.

"Aah! Aah!"

For the first time the creature made a noise. Jeremiah leapt off its back in surprise. It wasn't a sprite.

"It's you, thank God! I'm sorry. Are you okay?" Jeremiah could have hugged her. He felt overwhelmed with relief.

Shae-nae was dazed. She sat on the floor and looked up at him. He looked terrible, really pale despite his dark skin. He was almost grey.

"I thought you were that thing, I was trying to escape."

Shae-nae looked at the bedpan he was clutching. "It wouldna' worked anyway. I 'ad ta cut its 'ead off."

"How did you get here?"

"I just told ya, I cut that creatures 'ead off."

"No, I mean here, this place, this castle."

"I dunno, I can't remember. Wait, yeah, I wos runnin' from somink… no it was someone. I wasn't runnin' long, and then there wos a bang and a flash of light and…"

They heard the slam of a distant door. They both had a feeling something was coming.

"Let's get out of here, quick!"

The corridors were the same both ways: they stretched infinitely in opposite directions. Jeremiah followed Shae-nae.

"I saw the light too," he said, but Shae-nae did not reply.

They ran and ran but the corridor didn't end. They wouldn't give up though. Shae-nae looked behind. She was expecting something to be chasing them at least. There was nothing, nothing behind them and nothing in front of them. They were thirsty. Their throats rasped. They had to stop.

"What about them creatures?" Shae-nae panted. "They're scary 'aint they?"

Jeremiah was nodding.

"Every time that fing came into me room it made me relive stuff I'd tried ta forget, 'orrible stuff. It wos like mental torture every time I looked at it."

Jeremiah was nodding but he was panting too much to reply. His sprite had reminded him of stuff too. But worse than that, he felt as though it knew all of his secrets.

"What the…"

Shae-nae didn't finish. It happened too fast. Jeremiah didn't even have time to look up before the light consumed them both.

10

*H*e was in a... *cave?* Light was scarce. A few torches flickered on the distant mud coloured walls. A dark ceiling arched up into... it was too black to tell. He'd lost Shae-nae again, but this time Jeremiah was not alone. He watched the strange creatures queuing in the gloomy light. They were creatures the like of which he had never before seen or even imagined. They made him afraid. He wished Shae-nae were by his side still. She was strong. She of all people could help him find a way out. But she was gone. Instead there were these creatures, jostling, snarling, shouting, all different, foreign: alien. Single file they trudged past him as he lay on the floor recovering from his stupor. They were queuing endlessly for a spot of white light in the distance. They were wrapped in thick blanket like cloaks. Jeremiah realised he was cold and he shivered as he watched them. They didn't seem to notice him.

The creatures were ugly, slimy. Their features were bumpy. They had protuberances where humans didn't, but they stood and shuffled along the queue as humans would. They carried tools, in their strange stumpy hands.

Somehow Jeremiah knew the tools were weapons. It occurred to Jeremiah that he should join the queue. It might take him somewhere and he liked the look of the light. He stood. His knees almost buckled but he steadied himself, then he pushed into the queue.

"Aragamap! Aragamap nuio dchiki mazxctad."

Jeremiah felt his scalp burn. His feet left the ground. Then he landed roughly on the floor, crumpled. He turned and saw a tall creature snarling at him. Juices dripped from its stubby grey teeth and it had a tuft of his curly black hair in its strange stubby hand. Some of the creatures seemed to find him amusing. Others snarled like his aggressor. None approached him. Then they ignored him again. Jeremiah figured they didn't like queue jumpers. He thought he had better find the end of the queue.

He hadn't been walking long before he heard her voice.

"Psst! Jezza, it's me Shae-nae."

Jeremiah stared at the figures in the queue. He could not see her. He had expected her to be easy to spot amongst the alien creatures. Suddenly an arm reached out towards him. The blanket came away from the face.

"Shae-nae!" Jeremiah blinked away his tears of relief hoping she had not noticed them. He envied her there. She was fitting in. She was in the queue. She had a blanket. She was warm.

"Come over 'ere mate. Stand next ta me."

"How d'you get in?"

"I followed it round ta the end and just tagged along."

"I can't see the end, it goes on for miles."

"There didn't seem ta be so many of 'em when I first arrived."

"Where d'you get the blanket?"

"I found a sprite. His froat 'ad bin slit. I reckoned he wouldn't be needin' this any more." The blanket was blood stained where she'd wrapped it around her head.

"Is that your blood?"

"Whadd'ya mean?"

"The blood?" Jeremiah pointed to her forehead. She touched it. It felt sticky. She seemed surprised.

"I dunno'. I fought it wos the sprite's blood."

"It looks like yours. It looks fresh."

"I feel all right, well all rightish," Shae-nae shrugged.

Jeremiah frowned. She didn't look all right. She looked very pale, paler even than before and her lips were almost blue.

Some of the creatures turned and began to growl at them. Jeremiah squeezed into the queue next to Shae-nae. When he woke up he was on the floor again. The queue was still there but Shae-nae had gone. Alone again, Jeremiah fought his despair. Aching all over he decided to find the end of the queue and join it. It might lead him back to Shae-nae.

*

Shae-nae hoped Jeremiah was all right. She shouldn't have asked him to join her. She should have known they wouldn't like it. It had taken her hours to find the end of the queue and then it had moved so slowly. No wonder they didn't like queue jumpers. At the very least she should have told him to be quick if he saw a dead creature. He needed a blanket and a weapon, but the sprites were quick clearing the bodies up. No sooner was a creature dead than a sprite appeared and tidied its body away. She had been lucky, the creature her sprite had tried to clear away hadn't been dead and it had killed the sprite. Nothing came to clear the sprite up so she had its stuff. Jeremiah probably wouldn't have to wait very long for an opportunity. While she queued the creatures brutally murdered each other with increasing frequency using their strange weapons. Whatever was at the end of the queue was highly prized.

Shae-nae clutched the dead sprite's weapon tightly. She had been lucky to find it. It would come in handy. She carried it in her hand just as they did which felt strange: she would normally conceal a weapon. If Jeremiah had any sense he'd find the end of the queue join it and meet her near the light. She'd wait, as long as she could.

*

Jeremiah watched the fight break out. A tall rangy creature was bludgeoning another smaller creature to death. He wished he hadn't looked up just at the moment when the victim's eyes rolled back in its head just before it spun and crashed to the floor with a strange gurgling sound in its throat. There was so much liquid. It didn't look like human blood but he knew it was their equivalent. The body twitched horribly for ages. It turned his stomach. The sprite appeared and began clearing up the body. Jeremiah realised he was too late to grab the blanket and weapon.

The queue curled round and round. The cave like place was darker now. Some of the creatures had lanterns. Jeremiah seemed to be going down. Down. Lights flickered everywhere. Even above him. He looked down and realised the flickering queue spiralled for miles and miles, down and down. There was no end. He'd been walking for hours. He'd seen numerous deaths but he couldn't give up. He was drawn to the light at the other end. He could still see it even from this distance. He needed to get to it. He needed to join the queue, he felt as though his life depended on getting to the light. Jeremiah decided he needed a weapon; it would help when the time was right to push into the queue.

The creatures had been killing each other frequently since he'd seen Shae-nae many hours before, so he knew it would happen again soon. He didn't have to wait long. He'd be prepared this time. Loud snarling noises caught his attention. The argument was between three, then four, creatures. Jeremiah waited. He was waiting for one of them to die. He was banking on it. He didn't want to watch so he turned and waited to hear the thud of a body on the ground. There were two thuds: two bodies. The sprites appeared before he got there even though he was close. They weren't interested in him as they tidied the strange looking limbs over the creatures' chests, so Jeremiah took a cloak and both sets of weapons. At last he was warm and the weapons were good. One was a large claw with five prongs curved like arthritic fingers, the other looked like a serrated machete. He'd seen countless blunt weapons that required much force to be effective. He'd been lucky to get these. These were good, sharp: lethal.

Now that he had the weapons he decided he was going to jump the queue, he couldn't stand to be in the cold dark cave any longer than he had to. Jeremiah prowled along the queue looking for a cluster of small, weak creatures. He wanted to increase his odds of success and picking on the larger creatures would be folly. He felt it necessary to disguise his human features so he pulled the blanket round his head and then he barged into the queue.

"Aragamap, uchuro. Aragamap!" the nearest creature squawked.

Jeremiah felt a short sharp punch in the back of his shoulder. He pulled the blanket even further over his face. He did not turn around, hunching his shoulders instead and standing his ground.

"Aragamap duneo jinkle xosster."

The creature laid a stump on Jeremiah's shoulder.

Jeremiah felt his heart pounding but he still didn't turn around. He clutched his weapons tightly until his knuckles were white. The creature shook him even harder. It prodded him in the waist with something cold, hard. Jeremiah turned and viewed the creature submissively from under the shadow of his cloak. The creature seemed taken aback but its anger did not abate and it tried to wrestle Jeremiah out of the queue. Jeremiah looked up and saw the queue spiralling forever, disappearing into the distance. He couldn't lose this fight. He must stand his ground.

"Gyinu choul'd gnot gree weres," the creature squawked again.

Jeremiah shrugged and turned away but this time the creature grabbed his shoulders and forcibly turned him round.

"Gyiny chou'd gnot gree weres," it was snarling now.

Jeremiah didn't understand. He was scared. He panicked. He didn't know what he was doing but he knew he didn't want to lose his place in the queue. It was blind panic that made him do it. The creature suddenly stumbled backwards. It was afraid of him. A strange liquid was seeping between stumps that were once fingers as it clutched the gash in its stomach. Jeremiah's machete had gone in easily but he'd had to twist it to pull it out. At last the creature fell. Its eyes were fixed on Jeremiah. Jeremiah didn't know if it was dead or not. He thought it might get up and attack him; he thought the other creatures might attack him, but they were looking the other way, it was none of their business they just wanted to get to the light.

Jeremiah knew the creature was dead when the sprite appeared and tucked in its limbs neatly before dragging it off. Both sprite and victim seemed to just merge into the background. Considering it was his first kill he felt strangely numb, but he'd secured his place, he was in the queue and now he was heading towards the light.

There was something about the light that drew Jeremiah to it. It was blinding and although it was blinding he was able somehow to look at it and appreciate in detail its beauty. It radiated out from its source towards him trying to reach him, as though each tendril of light was a limb with fingers, elongated and elegant beckoning him towards it. He knew he had to reach it. If he had to kill all the creatures to get there he would. Jeremiah turned to the creature in front. He pulled its cloak roughly. It turned in anger and raised a claw. Jeremiah got to it first. He was quicker, keener, more determined. It was a clean kill and so he moved up the queue, the light pulling him towards it as though he were a moth. Sometimes he slipped between their stumpy legs; sometimes he killed them, but all so swiftly he felt as though he were running.

11

Shae-nae gagged as she wiped the putrid slime from her face. The creature behind her had squealed before its juices sprayed her. Its throat had been slit by another cloaked figure. Now the murderer was directly behind her. She gripped her weapon tightly. She would be ready if the murderer tried anything with her. The creature laid its stumpy hand on her shoulder. She froze. She tried not to react while she thought what to do.

"Uramanaxa chutranay hujoula."

Shae-nae shrugged in response but did not turn around. The creature shook her more firmly.

"Uramanaxa chutranay hujoula," it hissed again.

"Get lost freak," she hissed back, then she cringed expecting a blow. If it spoke again she would kill it before it killed her.

"Agarampamina hinchura guntwinc." Now the creature in front turned to face her. Its face was in shadow but its breath was warm and foul on her face. "Impacubala spinchiu de ji," it screeched and raised the weapon in its stubby hand.

Shae-nae saw the dull steal blades enlivened by the

blood of others. "They're going to kill me," she said, but she didn't know if she spoke out loud.

Suddenly there was a scream and the creature behind her fell to the floor. It squirmed around her ankles. Then it was dead. The creature in front gave a triumphant snort as the sprite dragged the victim away and then it turned its attention back to her. Shae-nae understood its threatening expression and without wasting any time she grabbed its throat before it could act against her. She thrust her weapon into the creature's torso but her weapon got stuck, she couldn't withdraw it. They were locked together by her weapon. The creature's cold blood spilled out over her hand and its hood slipped away so that the horror of its face was revealed. A tongue emerged from a grey fold in its face and like liquid seeped towards her, searching for her eyes; it was going to kill her, suck out her eyes with its strange liquid tongue.

There was a sudden flash of blade. Whatever it was missed her. There was another scream, a gargle. It was the first time she'd felt real terror, the terror of imminent death. Suddenly the creature she was locked together with fell to the floor. It hadn't killed her, something else got to it first. A sprite appeared and began dragging its body away. Shae-nae was unsure what had happened. She was in shock.

"Are you alright?"

It took a while to realise someone was talking to her in a language she recognised. An arm was around her shoulder. It felt good.

"Shae-nae it's me Jeremiah."

She didn't know who he was. He shook her shoulders and slapped her face. Her eyes seemed to focus.

"Shae-nae it's me. It's me Jeremiah. You were nearly a gonna."

Shae-nae was silent as she took in his soiled cloak, his sharp eyes, his purposeful, dangerous expression. He looked tough, tougher than before, and his face seemed keener: she could see the man he was going to be.

"Keep walking." He grabbed her elbow and she allowed him to lead her. She wanted him to lead her towards the light. He was taking control and he was making her feel safe. "I remembered something back there, something significant," he continued. "I remembered having an accident. A car hit me just before I came here. Up until then I didn't understand why I was queuing for the light. It just felt like an instinct and I just knew I had to obey it. Getting to the light seemed, still seems, more important than anything I've ever done before, as though my life depends on it. That light is my life."

Shae-nae was nodding. It felt like that for her too. Her nerves, her energy, adrenalin, all were on red alert, working at maximum intensity to get her to the light.

"Then I remembered the accident and realised that's exactly what we are doing."

Shae-nae spoke at last: "What d'ya mean?"

"Keep walking." Jeremiah pulled her sleeve. "We're

fighting for our lives," he whispered as though he didn't want the other creatures to know. "That's why those creatures were trying to kill us, and each other. They all want to reach the light first."

"I dahn't understand."

"Don't you feel it pulling you towards it?"

Shae-nae nodded.

"It's like an instinct isn't it? You can't get away from it." Jeremiah pointed towards it. "Look at it, it's beautiful, it's worth fighting for isn't it?"

"I feel as though I'll die if I dahn't get there. I've never wanted anyfink more in my life," Shae-nae agreed.

"The light *is* life Shae-nae. It's our ticket out of here."

"Outta' where? I still dahn't know where the 'ell we are."

"Hell is right. Damn right. Don't you see it yet?" It was an appeal. He wanted her to work it out for herself. He'd never been good with bad news.

Shae-nae shook her head, exasperated. "I dahn't know what ya' talkin' about. It's like ya' mad or somink." She was afraid of him suddenly.

"Shae-nae, we're dead."

"What!"

"Reaching the light is the only way out of here, back to life, that's why they're killing each other. They're all fighting for a chance to go home, to have another shot at life."

84

Shae-nae reeled. She felt as though she needed to sit, to feel something supporting her body, but she was in a place devoid of comfort.

"What happened to you immediately before you found yourself in that room in the castle?" Jeremiah continued.

Shae-nae could barely think straight but she forced herself to relive what she could remember.

"I was at home. I…I dunno' I just remember followin' a light. Yeah, followin' a light like this one, 'cept I was at home."

"Me too. I followed one down our driveway. I don't remember why. It was weird but I just couldn't stop myself, and the next thing I remember I was waking up here. Shae-nae I think we died. You've got all that blood on your head. You're so pale."

Shae-nae was stunned, but it seemed so shockingly clear all of a sudden. Jeremiah's neck was all twisted and one shoulder was hanging down unnaturally. There was blood all over his clothes and he was so yellow. She knew then she'd been talking to a corpse. Jeremiah was dead and that meant she was too. "Oh my god, me mum!"

It was the first time Jeremiah had seen her cry. He didn't know she was crying because she believed her mother wouldn't care that she was dead. The tears came and melted the dried blood that covered one side of her face. She could smell it, her own blood, as though it were fresh.

"Shae-nae, you've got to get a grip. That light is our ticket out of here. We died before our time. We're getting a chance to go back. I told you I think I was hit by a car. You must have had a head injury. You've so much blood on your head and down your face."

Shae-nae held onto his arm. She remembered the bang that came just before she'd seen the light for the first time. She remembered the pain, she wasn't sure that it had ever gone away, only that she'd got more used to it.

"Look the main thing is we feel all right, so even if we are dead, that's something isn't it? Now we get a chance to go back through this light!"

Jeremiah was afraid she was losing it. She'd been so strong up until now. He had been depending on her strength but now she was exhausted and now it was time for her to depend on him.

"Shae-nae focus on the light. Don't let anything else distract you. We have got to get to that light and we can do it together, even if we have to kill every single one of these freaky monsters that are in our goddamned way."

He was right. She wanted to get to the light at whatever cost. And although she wasn't ready to admit it she knew he was right about them being dead. And what she knew more than any of those things was that she didn't want to be dead. They had to focus on the light: they had to get to the light.

Shae-nae reached for Jeremiah's hand but it was not his she felt. She turned. He was gone. She did not feel despair though: she felt nothing. Her emotions were on hold as she wondered whose hand it was that gripped her as tightly as she gripped theirs. She turned again and saw that the hand belonged to her sprite. This time her sprite did not conjure up dark memories, this time when Shae-nae looked at her sprite she was reminded of her baby cousin Sky and happy memories of her sweet cherubic face flooded back. It was one of only a few happy memories that Shae-nae had. She could almost hear the little baby girl giggling as she remembered pushing her gently in a swing. Shae-nae felt her heart swell with happiness as it did during those times with the little baby girl; and that feeling of happiness even though it was only ever fleeting, reminded her of her desire to survive. In that brief moment Shae-nae was invincible.

The light was suddenly upon Shae-nae. The sprite yanked her hand painfully, pulling her right into it. She was blinded by the light and she jarred as though something like a bullet, hit her head and sent her reeling. Then she felt as though she was falling like a stone.

"Jeremiah!" she called but there was no answer.

12

*I*t was a while before Shae-nae realised the wetness on her face was no longer her own tears. She had run out of tears long ago. The glowing white walls of the tube that had curved around her were suddenly gone and greyness surrounded her instead. The warm wind that had carried her along the tube turned cool and made her want to hug herself tightly and pull on a jumper. She was no longer floating, nor was she inside the strange brightly lit tube anymore. The wetness on her face was rain and she was standing on something green, it was green grass, a small sparse patch of it. The ghostly laughter that had rung in her ears and made her despair had become words, actual words that belonged to real voices. Goose pimples pricked her skin all over because she was sure that she had just heard men saying words that defied belief; belief in the world as she knew it.

Shae-nae was squatting behind a wheelie bin. There were two men, both tall, both handsome, although one incredibly so. The more handsome one was much younger. Both wore expensive suits but they didn't seem to mind the rain. They were talking to Freddy. What was Freddy doing here in the tube? But she wasn't in the tube anymore she was surrounded by high rise council flats. Shae-nae wanted to call out to Freddy but something made her stop. Instead she watched him. The men were quizzing him. She could tell Freddy was pretending to be helpful but she knew him well enough to know he was also being cagey: Freddy always held things back.

"Have you seen her?" one of the men was asking. He gave Freddy a photo. Shae-nae couldn't help noticing how extremely well spoken both men were. They must be rich, she thought.

"Who wants ter knaa?" Freddy responded unhelpfully.

"We just want to help her that's all," the other man said softly, but there was something about the way he said it that made her afraid. "Her name is Sharnay," he added smiling.

Shae-nae stopped breathing momentarily. They were looking for her. But who were they? She'd never seen them before. Freddy was right not to trust them, she thought.

"Shae-nae yer mean, she dahn't need no ones 'elp," Freddy replied.

"So you do know her then?"

Freddy paused, realising he'd said too much: "Nah mate, made a mistake, never seen 'er before in me life."

But Freddy's cockiness disintegrated and he quailed as the barrel of a large handgun was shoved under his nose.

"Are you sure about that?" the first man asked.

Suddenly Freddy panicked and bolted. He was running as fast as he could over the square towards the rec. It was less than two seconds before Shae-nae heard a bang. She watched Freddy drop to the ground like a stone. A pool of red formed on the back of his shirt and spilled onto the ground around him.

"A bit hasty," the first man remarked to the second man who was still pointing the gun.

"He wasn't going to tell us anything."

"He would have cracked. He was a coward."

The more handsome man nodded in agreement. "But we didn't need him anymore. He knew her well. We're close."

Shae-nae was trembling behind the wheelie bin. She was trying to think of another person named Shae-nae that they could have been looking for but she didn't know anyone named Shae-nae but herself. They were looking for her. Why? She'd paid her dues; she didn't owe anyone anything as far as she could remember; she'd really been trying to get her act together.

They were coming towards her now. The handsome man was still wielding the gun. She was sure they didn't know she was hiding behind the wheelie bin, but they were getting closer, walking straight towards her. God, *did* they know she was there? Could they see through the bin? Shae-nae began to panic. Their ever-nearing presence was becoming evermore suffocating. Suddenly Shae-nae panicked. She stood up quickly, tipping the bin over and she ran. She knew without looking that they had spotted her, and were chasing her. There was another bang and almost immediately she felt a sharp pain as though something had glanced the side of her head.

"There she is. Get her!"

Shae-nae turned and saw the two men running towards her, their faces were shadowed with evil intent. She burst into a sprint. She was confused and disorientated: a second ago she'd been floating in that tunnel now even though her legs were still weak like that of a newborn lamb, she was running for her life.

A tall grey building with countless windows obscured by tat loomed above her. Instinctively she ran towards it because it felt familiar to her somehow. There were double doors at the bottom, so she ran through them. At least she was sheltered from the rain now, so what was the warm wet liquid trickling down her face over her ear? Her head throbbed and it felt light, as though she were leaving herself and floating away. The hallway was dark and dingy. The woes of countless discontented souls had been poured out from spray cans and were decorating its grim walls. Shae-nae wanted to get away from the men but also the words on the wall: they were explicit and frightening, reminding her of many terrible nightmares she tried to forget.

There was another set of double doors straight ahead. They were cold and grey and also decorated. They were uninviting but she ran towards them anyway. She pressed the button to call the lift even though somehow she knew the lift wouldn't come, just as she knew beating the smashed plastic button repeatedly wouldn't make it come any faster, it would just make her fingers sore. She heard footsteps, and heavy breathing outside on the path. Shae-nae began punching the button until her hands were sore. The men were coming but the lift wasn't. The doors behind her opened with an uncharacteristically graceful swish as the men approached. They were coming for her. Why had she run in? She cursed herself for getting trapped, she should have legged it through the estate, she could have disappeared over the rec and jumped across the railway line. Yes, she would have had a much better chance of escape.

Suddenly Shae-nae realised how she knew all these things about the place. She was home. She'd followed the light and come home. But this was not how she wanted it to be. Freddy was dead and two men were chasing her with a gun.

"In there," one of the men snapped. They were coming through the doors. The lift was taking too long. Shae-nae headed for the stairs instead. She was only vaguely aware of climbing them and was relieved when she reached the floor where her mother's flat was. She thumped on the door. Was her mother in? There was no reply. Shae-nae remembered her key suddenly. She'd forgotten that she had one in her pocket because it was as though she had to re-learn her memories again. Now the key was in her shaky hands as she fumbled at the lock.

"There she is," one of the men called.

Shae-nae fell into the flat and kicked the door shut. The men were thudding on it behind her, an incessant violent banging. *The phone!* She had to get to the phone before they kicked the door in; but she was panicking because she kept visualising the phone knocked over on the floor and out of reach, as though it was a nightmare she'd had many times over. Shae-nae shook the negative image from her brain. She had to act fast because somehow she knew they were going to kick the door in. 'How did she know that?' she asked herself? But the answer to that question didn't matter now, she just had to get to the phone and tell the police what she'd heard, explain why the men were chasing her.

Shae-nae stumbled into the living room where her mother was slumped on a chair. The television was blaring but her mother's eyes were shut and a thread of dibble connected the corner of her mouth to a dark patch on the arm of the chair.

"Mum!" mum would deal with the men now, she hoped. Weak with relief and fatigue, Shae-nae fell to her knees and began shaking her mother to wake her. "Help me mum," she cried through an explosion of tears. "They're gonna' finish me off. I 'eard some stuff I shouldn'a. Mum? Mum?" Shae-nae shook her harder but her mother was unmoving. "Mum! Fa God's sake they're gonna' kill me! D'ya 'ear me? They're gonna' kill me!"

Shae-nae wailed. Her mother was in another drunken stupor. She was unconscious again. Just this once Shae-nae had believed that her mother might be able to help her, embrace her at least and tell her everything would be okay even if it wasn't going to be. In the face of her daughter's imminent murder, surely at last she would spring into action and be the mother Shae-nae craved. Shae-nae groaned. Her mother was crap: a useless drunk. Shae-nae was alone as always.

The banging on the door grew louder more violent. They were kicking it in. She knew they would be upon her soon. With a last concentration of her remaining energy, Shae-nae dived for the telephone. She knocked over the flimsy table and the handset landed out of reach. She knew it would happen: she knew she wasn't going to escape. The door flew open and the men with guns stood over her with strange expressions: sorrowful, yet purposeful. She'd been here before and somehow she knew what would happen next. She closed her eyes. There was a bang. It was over.

*

The warm air was still washing over him but the blinding light had gone. Instead there was a natural light, the sort of light Jeremiah had yearned for since finding himself in that place. It was daylight. Jeremiah was crouching on the ground. The ground was green and he realised that it was

94

grass, sweet smelling, luscious grass, the like of which he could only have dreamed of when he was in that place. The terrifying whispers that seemed to have followed him down the tube of light had been replaced by the magical sound of rustling leaves caused by the same mild summer wind that stroked his face. He was beneath a tree: a tree exactly like the one he had at home outside his bedroom window. He turned to view his bedroom window and his heart skipped a beat as he spotted his navy check curtains flapping in the breeze. He was home, home at last. The magic of it took his breath away. He hadn't realised how happy he should have been until he lost everything and became a prisoner in that place. He shuddered to think how he had found himself there, with those creatures. It didn't matter now though, he was home. He stood and called out to his father to let him know that he was home, but there was no answer.

Jeremiah headed for the house. The front door opened for him as though it were expecting him. He stepped into the hallway. His soft trainers clicked on the cold marble floor. There was no one home but he was not disappointed, somehow he had known there wouldn't be. The door to his father's office was open and Jeremiah was drawn towards it even though he feared the room beyond.

The room was large, the furniture expensive. It occurred to Jeremiah that he had not known this before; he had never been in his father's office and seen all the strange artefacts that reeked of dark purpose. Standing in the doorway like an uninvited guest he spotted a laptop sitting in the middle of a large ebony desk. The laptop was switched on. Jeremiah felt it beckon him over. He never could resist the lure of a computer. Feeling suddenly nervous he turned around expecting someone to be standing behind him trying to catch him out. The warm feeling of happiness he had felt at being home was suddenly gone and he felt afraid. He didn't want to feel afraid but he did want to look at the laptop. A memory of his father's warning suddenly rang in his ears: *"Don't ever go in my office son, d'ya hear me, EVER!"* Jeremiah looked over his shoulder again, but his father was not there. There was only silence, silence except for the sound of the gentle breeze coming through the window.

Jeremiah tiptoed across the room. Pushing the black leather chair out of the way – he didn't dare sit: sitting would make him feel as though he was staying and he didn't intend to be long, just long enough- he swiped his fingers over the silky touch pad and the starry screen saver disappeared.

THE HOLE: CONFIDENTIAL REPORT
Contents:
1/ Predicted growth in sales of Heaven Sent Perpetuity Bonds (HSPB's) over a 10 year period.

2/ Predicted profits over the same period.

3/ Presidential campaign strategy.

4/ Election and beyond...

Feeling uneasy, Jeremiah looked behind him again, but there was nothing there. He looked back at the screen. He didn't understand what he was reading. Was his father campaigning to be President? He'd never said anything. Jeremiah wanted to read more. He clicked on *'CONFIDENTIAL REPORT'*. Nothing happened. He clicked on 'THE HOLE' but it took him to his father's homepage, so he clicked back and returned to the message. Jeremiah read it again. He wondered what a 'Heaven Sent Perpetuity Bond' could be. He clicked on the words. A curser flashed on a white screen and the word 'Password' appeared next to a box. Jeremiah decided to pull up the chair after all. He sat down. He could do this. He'd just been expelled from school for doing this sort of thing. He considered himself a professional hacker.

He was not impressed by his father's security: he cracked the code quickly using only a basic formula. Jeremiah wondered if his father understood how inadequate the security was. An egg timer prompted Jeremiah to wait, something was happening. The screen changed. It became black. A red strip started to fill the loading bar. 'Please wait', said the message. Then there was music, strange eerie, unreal music, and dollar signs appeared next to stars.

"Please enter your three digit star code."

What's a star code? Jeremiah wondered. He looked around the room, not knowing at first that the room itself would yield a clue. The stuffed head of a lion mounted on the wall looked back at him with glassy eyes despite its mouth being set as though it was roaring furiously. It was freaky, Jeremiah didn't like it. Then he noticed that the room was full of lion motifs: a proud lion was carved into the desk; lions were carved all over the solid gold cigar box; a huge painting of a pride of lions dominated by a male was mounted on the wall; and a fantastic bronze of a female and her cubs stood proudly on an elaborate glass pedestal. Lions! His father's birthday: his father's star sign. Jeremiah typed the word 'LEO' into the box. Another egg timer appeared. Something was happening. It was all too easy.

There was new music, still eerie, but this time it was subdued background music. Jeremiah looked over his shoulder again; he felt edgy and imagined eyes were boring into the back of his head. Still there was nobody there. He turned back to the computer screen. It looked completely black at first but something began stirring in its centre, some sort of ultra blackness with a thin whisker of light around it. It took Jeremiah's breath away.

"Welcome Master."

A ghostly voice startled him suddenly and he came out in goose bumps. Jeremiah was scared. *What was this stuff?* He felt again as though someone were watching him. He turned to face the door. Was that the flicker of a shadow? No, there was nothing, no shadow, just silence; his nerves were getting the better of him. He turned to face the computer screen again. Suddenly there was a chime and the ultra blackness was overwritten. An icon appeared that looked like an unopened scroll.

"You have one new message," the ghostly voice sang.

With his heart in his mouth Jeremiah clicked on the icon. He felt tense, excited, afraid. Quickly the screen was filled with the face of the most beautiful woman. Jeremiah felt his stomach flip with excitement as he admired her glossy black hair, and her black eyes, like deep dark holes. She was so beautiful that if Jeremiah hadn't actually met Iman Khan in the flesh he might have wondered if the image before him was real or animated. But she was real, and the video message was real.

Iman Khan's face was in dark shadow until she held the lamp up beside her face. In the lamplight her eyes seemed to spark like embers in a draught. She appeared to be broadcasting the message from inside a dark cave.

"We found the final cave. The Babylonia site 6X reveals all. It is as we expected, look!" she said. Her voice echoed as she swung the lamp around the walls of the cave which looked orange in the glow of the lamp. The walls were decorated with strange blocks of black text written in a language Jeremiah could neither read nor recognise, and there were paintings too. One of the pictures directly behind Iman was of a city. He didn't know what the black circle in the middle of the city was supposed to be. It looked as though the people had dug a big Hole.

"The missing pieces of the story are found," Iman said

excitedly. The city disappeared suddenly. Iman had moved and was holding the lamp up next to a portrait. "There he is," Iman pointed excitedly. A dark and beautiful face was illuminated. Thick black make up gave drama to the piercingly green eyes. The face was noble and powerful… and strangely familiar. The face both frightened and mesmerised Jeremiah.

"Eviathan," Iman said as though the name meant something. "Look how regal he is. So beautiful, you must agree, don't let modesty stand in the way of truth." Iman smiled at the portrait again before swinging the lamp towards the next portrait. The next portrait was of a woman. Iman could barely disguise her contempt. "Katchua, the cause of all our problems," was all she said before moving onto the portrait of another man and woman, both dressed in elaborately painted blue gowns. The man was older, crooked, but strong looking, the woman younger, incredibly beautiful and with the darkest and coldest eyes. The portrait looked just like Iman. Jeremiah felt cold suddenly and shivered. It was as if those eyes were looking right out of the computer screen at him.

"Tanimesh and Ganyshere," Iman announced. "Look at Ganyshere, I never fail to be amazed by her beauty even if I do say so myself. Their lives are entwined with ours; we are bound together by the Hole, and look at this." Iman raised the lamp up to another picture. This time it looked more like a sketch. Four identical matchstick children lay in a row. One had a cross through it, but all had their eyes closed as though they were dead. Jeremiah thought the sketch was eerie, creepy even.

"This," Iman said, pointing at the picture, "should look like this." With exaggerated effort she began to scratch a cross over each of the remaining three figures. Then she threw her head back and laughed, the lamp light projecting her sinister black shadow onto the wall of the cave behind her.

"We will be rid of Katchua's children soon. But now you must go," she said, as if to him, even though Jeremiah knew the message was meant for his father. "You must go at once to England. The translations are correct. Look!" Iman pointed at another glyph excitedly. There was a painting of a dark lake and behind it a mountain. The mountain looked sinister and bore a deep black scar across its face. Next to it was the picture of a girl. The girl had a fairy tale quality about her. Iman's eyes widened and they darkened beyond nature.

"It is her. Look, this is the mountain and this is the lake. I lost the Hole when it broke through into our atmosphere; it travelled at a speed our best technology could not follow. But Bill always said it would be so, he always knew, even before we found this cave. He was right. The Hole has come for her. The Hole is in this lake," she pointed at the lake in the painting. "And this lake, this mountain, and this girl are in England," she finished. "Once she is destroyed the 'Hole' will be all yours. The world will be yours my love, all yours! *Imagine!*" Her eyes were glistening with intensity as though they were about to burst into flames.

Jeremiah's heart felt sick suddenly. He was frightened. Why would Iman Khan, an expert astrophysicist, be mooching around in some dingy cave in Iraq of all places? The way she crossed out those figures in that sketch was nothing short of sinister, and the bit about destroying the girl...

Somehow Jeremiah knew Iman Khan was saying something bad even though he didn't understand what it was. It all seemed to have something to do with a Hole but what could be so exciting about a Hole? Jeremiah suddenly felt overwhelmed and uncertain. He didn't want to be in his home anymore, it didn't feel like his home anymore. The message made him want to run away, far away. He ran for the door. The doorway was blocked. Levi Washington towered over his son. His expression was grim.

"I'm sorry you had to see that son."

Jeremiah said nothing: he could not think of anything to say. This wasn't how it was supposed to be. This wasn't what he was expecting when he followed the light and came home from that place. It was all wrong, even his father's face... Except for his piercing green eyes, his father's features were blurred; Jeremiah couldn't make them out clearly no matter how he tried. But he knew it was his father and his father seemed like a devil.

"Don't be afraid son." Jeremiah's father extended a hand and came forward. He placed his hand on Jeremiah's shoulder and gripped it tightly... too tightly. Without ever understanding why, Jeremiah had feared his father since he could first remember. But in that gesture of the outstretched hand, the taut smile, and the tight grip on his shoulder, Jeremiah suddenly understood everything about his father that had always made him afraid: his control, his power, his cool indifference to his son. As he looked at his father's tight mouth unused to smiling, he could see clearly his father's ambition; such a dark ambition that would destroy anything, even his own son. That's when Jeremiah decided to run. Taking his father by surprise he twisted his shoulder free, ducked from his other grasping hand, ran towards the window and dived out of it.

It was dark again. He hadn't noticed it getting dark. Dark or not he had to run, run away from the house, run away from his father. He could hear the heavy boots of his father crunching down the gravel driveway, gaining on him. Jeremiah felt his panic choking him. *His own father!* He was left in no doubt that his own father wanted to kill him. He'd been here before.

Suddenly there was light. Jeremiah ran towards the light although he didn't understand why. The light got bigger, brighter, it illuminated the gravel driveway before him, and the night darkened grass became green again. He kept running until he was out of breath. He hadn't expected to hear a car engine roar. It confused him so he stopped running. The engine roared again. Jeremiah stared into the two parallel beams as the engine roared for a third and final time. The wheels screeched. The gravel crunched and the light came towards him. Suddenly he didn't want to be near the light but there was nowhere for him to go. He shielded his eyes from the brightness. Then a shower of light blinded him.

Jeremiah felt as though he were floating, and could see everything from above as though he were in the trees. He could see his father's dark skin and his golden front tooth glinting in the lights from the car headlamps as he headed towards a boy. The boy was lying on the ground now. One shoulder was twisted unnaturally and he was still shielding his face with his arms even after the light had passed. Jeremiah closed his eyes. He knew he was the boy on the grass, and he knew he was dead.

13

*I*t was cold. The snow swirled incessantly. The wind carried clouds of it into drifts and the ground was obscured with a cold white blanket. Darkness had fallen. Jeremiah watched the silent flakes coming towards him. He shivered. He was cold... and he was wondering why his father had killed him. The light in the tunnel had replayed his murder to him as though it were a scene from a movie before dumping him back in that place again. Jeremiah couldn't help replaying the memory over and over. It made him cry out. His father hadn't even flinched as the car engine roared towards flesh and blood that was his own. There had been no hesitation, no impulse to recall the order and prevent the murder of his son. How could he have looked so impassive as he stood over the mown down body of his own son? That hurt Jeremiah the most. It was as though his death was of no consequence.

Jeremiah sobbed into his cold hands. It seemed his father hadn't loved him. It seemed he preferred some damn Hole in the middle of a lake in England somewhere. His own father had condemned him to this gloomy, terrifying and lonely place for seeing some stuff on his computer that he didn't even understand. The painful memory gripped Jeremiah's heart with a chill worse than all the ice and snow. Jeremiah cupped his face with his hands and sobbed again. He did not know how long he sobbed for.

Lying on his back and shivering in the freezing snow, Jeremiah watched the dark clouds obscuring the bright stars as they passed them, like a magician's cloak in a magic trick. His expression was glazed and he was too numb to appreciate the spectacular late show that nature was providing. As he lay there, he was only vaguely aware that his hands were burning with cold, but as the awareness grew stronger he was unable to fight the impulse to warm them. Jeremiah held his hands in front of his face and blew on them. He could see his frosty breath by the light of the moon and it was warm enough to make some impression upon his cold hands. He blew again as an owl hooted nearby. How bizarre, he thought, that he should have warm breath even though he was dead.

Suddenly Jeremiah sat bolt upright. Did dead people have breath let alone warm breath? Jeremiah blew into his hands again. Yes, he had warm breath. The owl hooted again. Jeremiah looked up at the tree where he thought the hoot was coming from, it wasn't an alien creature or a sprite, it was a perfectly normal sounding owl. If he wasn't in the castle this time he might be… Jeremiah blew his cold hands… no, there was no sense in giving himself false hope, of course he wasn't alive in this cold, dark place.

Lying down in the freezing snow though did not seem like such a good idea suddenly. Standing up, Jeremiah dusted the snow from his trousers, but he was well and truly soaked. He needed to get moving and warm up a bit. The notion that he might still be alive struck him again. This time it was like a lightening bolt and hope instinctively surged inside him. But he remembered so clearly his own death, it was difficult to imagine that he might still be alive. There was something about that light the creatures were fighting for. Maybe…? Jeremiah decided to suppress his excitement again, he owed it to self-preservation. Yet suppressed though it was, the idea that he was alive glowed in his heart like an ember waiting to be fanned into a blaze.

*

Freezing cold and soaking wet Jeremiah found some shelter from the biting wind and the heavy snow fall behind a thicket of tangled gorse. The gorse was so dense the snow hadn't really managed to penetrate it so the bracken underneath was still bare and fairly dry. Sitting down upon the bed of dead bracken Jeremiah thought about the lights he could see in the distance. The lights belonged to a dwelling of some description. It wasn't the castle, it was far too small. Perhaps it was somewhere he could take shelter and rest, dry off his freezing clothes. The landscape standing between him and the dwelling was fairly gentle and undulating, but everything was covered in deep snow, that was the real problem. He looked back towards the dwelling. Perhaps he might find Shae-nae inside warming herself by a fire, who knows. Then an image of a sprite handing Shae-nae a hot drugged drink flashed through his mind and he recoiled and groaned. That's when he heard voices.

Jeremiah looked out through the tangle of spiky branches and saw a dark figure looming towards him. He recoiled afraid, but he could still see the broad figure approaching. The figure seemed to be searching for something, searching in his direction. Had it heard him groan?

"Yer must be made o'ghost flesh. Thur can be no other explanation fer it," the creature said suddenly but it sounded tired and breathless.

Jeremiah was just wondering if ghost flesh was the same stuff the sprites were made from when he heard another voice, the voice of a girl.

"Yer knew I couldn't wait. It'd kill me ter wait."

"I didn't knaw such a thing and if I 'ad knawn I woulda' thrown yer in a cell wi' nowt more than some 'ot liquid fer company."

Jeremiah thought of the cells in the castle and he shuddered. The creature must be some sort of gaoler and the castle, even though he couldn't see it, must still be nearby.

"I would've escaped that an' all, so it wurn't worth yer while tryin'"

"Aye no doubt yer right. Yer made o' some right funny stuff yer are. I ain't never met another'un like yer."

"Aye, so don't bother tryin' ter keep us out o' this murderous business. Yer can't, they want me I told yer. They want me as much as our lad an' I can't be kept safe from 'em even if yer lock us up."

"Now then lassy don't be gettin' all daft about that business down by't lake again or... thur it goes again."

The gaoler fell silent suddenly. He was listening to the same terrible moaning sound that Jeremiah could hear right next to him somewhere. It was close by in the same thicket of gorse. Jeremiah couldn't see what terrible creature was making the noise through the dense mass of twigs and thorns but he was terrified all the same. He wanted to run away from it, but if he ran the gaoler would see him. He was trapped.

"What... what is it?" he heard the girl say. She sounded nervous, afraid.

"I keep 'earin' a groanin' noise like some wretched tortured soul. I think it's comin' from that gorse o'er thur," the gaoler said. "Stand back while I tekk a look."

The groaning of the tortured soul continued as the gaoler approached. Jeremiah sank back into the snow desperate to remain hidden from the strange gaoler heading towards him. The tortured soul, one of those creatures no doubt, made a prolonged low pitched moan; then a short burst of dry painful sounding coughing was followed by a squeal, as though some jolt of pain was inflicted. Jeremiah was afraid. He knew what happened in this place, murder was rife and nobody seemed able to tolerate anyone else, even that girl going on about the 'murderous business'. Maybe the tortured soul was an escapee, a wounded victim who they'd come to finish off. The crunching of the snow got louder as the gaoler approached. He was close. Now the gaoler's solid form was leaning over the thicket casting an even darker shadow. Shrinking back from him Jeremiah pulled the weapon from his cloak. He would use it if he had to.

14

*J*eremiah's heart was still pounding furiously in his chest. When the gaoler had loomed towards him he'd closed his eyes tightly, swiping blindly with the weapon so that he wasn't really sure whether he'd hurt the gaoler or not. Such was the force of his swipe that he'd twisted and fallen face down in the thorns.

It was only now as he lay face down, painfully gripped by a mass of twigs and thorns that he could see the horror of the thing that was groaning next to him. It was a dying sheep; its wide eyes communicating the agony of its cold and thorny death as it lay trapped in the gorse like a fly in a spider's web. Its tongue twitched in spasms. Its body was too weak to squirm in protest anymore even though Jeremiah could feel its will to do so. Suddenly, the meagre remains of its life expired in Jeremiah's face; its last warm breath touching his cheek. Jeremiah retched as he furiously rubbed the feel of the sheep's dying breath from his cheek.

Terrible pains suddenly began to crunch deep inside him and he began to feel faint. He fell out of the gorse and into the snow tearing his flesh free from the thorns; but it was the pain in his gut that overwhelmed him. The pain was getting stronger and Jeremiah began to writhe in the snow stifling his cries of agony. He felt a cold shadow pass over his tense curled up body. I'm dying again, he thought. Even his murder hadn't been this painful though. Just when Jeremiah thought he could stand the pain no longer and preyed for his death to end it, the pain stopped. But he was not dead, not the sort of dead he understood anyway. Jeremiah looked up and saw the gaoler staring down at him with an expression of disbelief, terror even. The gaoler's features were suddenly clear in the moonlight. They were normal features. The gaoler was a man. But a man with such fear etched upon his face as he looked at him. Then the man hastily turned and headed back to the girl blocking her from coming to take a look. Jeremiah could hear a vague mumbled explanation but he was pretty sure the man did not mention him to the girl. Jeremiah wondered what had become of him to make a man look at him as though he didn't believe what he was seeing.

*

Padding over the snow like a cat stalking a bird, and dropping to his belly if he thought the man and the girl might turn and see him, Jeremiah followed them; yet all the while he felt as though he were being stalked by something. Sometimes, just like a frightened cat he turned wildly, swiping the air with his weapon, but there was never anything there. He dismissed the feeling as paranoia. The strain of everything that had happened made him very jumpy and he was imagining things, as though a shadow not his own were following him.

Jermiah stopped and dropped to his belly again when the girl and the man came to a halt in front of the dwelling. It was a ramshackle cottage but the warm orange glow coming from the downstairs window made it look as though it was cosy inside. He desperately wanted to be inside but he heard the girl saying: "Maybe we shouldn't," and she was pulling on the man's coat as though trying to stop him getting closer to it.

"Now then Emily, I didn't come all this way ter look at yer front door, I'll be seein' what's on't other side. No doubt I'll enjoy a nice brew and then I'll be on me way."

So the girl was called Emily. A nice, safe, normal name, he thought. It was comforting to hear.

"No wait," she hissed anxiously. I'll wait back 'ere. Don't tell 'em I came back wi' yer just in case."

She seemed so fearful. It gave Jeremiah a sense of foreboding. He was back in a place where humans were nervous, afraid. He watched as the girl hopped over a crumbling wall that surrounded a small stone animal shelter. It was the first time he had a really good look at her face and Jeremiah felt a sudden flicker of recognition, but the feeling disappeared when she crouched down behind the wall and became hidden from view.

The man banged on the door. A woman opened it.

There were smiles. Jeremiah wondered why the girl had been so afraid. It wasn't long afterwards that she hopped over the wall and went inside.

Jeremiah decided to follow Emily's tracks and hide behind the same wall. From there he'd be able to watch the house from a safe distance; he could also take shelter in the old stone outbuildings. It would be better than sleeping in the elements although not so good as sleeping in the cottage. He shivered as he approached the wall. That shadow was behind him again, touching him it seemed, as though a spider was crawling across the back of his neck. He turned expecting to see someone: there was nothing. He shrugged and tightened his shoulders keeping them tightened and tense until he'd climbed over the old stone wall and was safely hidden behind it.

15

*I*t was a relief to see her mother opening the front door. Emily watched the pleasant exchange between her mother and PC Birkett and she couldn't help smiling when they did. Seeing her mother standing in the doorway so robust and so well, made all her problems seem a little out of proportion, as PC Birkett had indeed suggested. Her mother didn't look in the least bit worried about anything. Obviously, there was going to be a perfectly rational explanation for everything. Emily braced herself: that meant she was probably going to get a right telling off but, hey ho, if it meant Thomas was safe she didn't care.

"Ma!" Emily cried out without any further hesitation, and she clambered out from behind the wall. "Ma, I thought yer wur..." Emily didn't want to say what she thought.

Dot's smile faded: "Emily luv...what yer doin' 'ere? I thought yer wur..." her voice faltered, then tailed off.

"Right let's be 'avin yer then," said PC Birkett, ushering Emily through the door first. "Come on, mekk room ferus wi' yer Dot, anyone would think yer wurn't pleased ter 'ave yer lass 'ome again."

"Oh, Emily," Dot said again, and held her daughter tight to her bosom.

Being gripped so tightly made Emily feel on edge. Something was wrong.

"Now then Mrs 'Ayward, 'ow 'bout a nice 'ot brew? It's a wonder wur alive the adventure we've 'ad this night, what wi' weather, and comin' o'er Scar Fell like," said PC Birkett forcing everyone into the small hallway and closing the front door behind him.

The feeling that something wasn't right wouldn't leave Emily and she felt somehow, that it had been unwise for PC Birkett to close the front door so that they were all imprisoned in the hallway. Emily noticed the living room door was slightly ajar. Something was definitely wrong. She looked up again into her mother's face. Now she saw it. Now she saw something in her mother's face that PC Birkett was oblivious to, something resembling fear.

Quick as a flash Emily saw a flicker of a shadow moving behind the living room door. Somebody was behind it. For a split second she thought it might be Thomas and she gasped with excitement, but Dot sensing her excitement squeezed her even harder. It was a warning. Emily turned to face PC Birkett, as though with her expression alone she could make him understand that he needed to open the front door, the escape route, but he was oblivious to her attempts at telepathy. Besides he wasn't even looking at her, he was looking beyond her, his hearty smile draining from

116

his face. Feeling the hairs prickle on the back of her neck, Emily turned to see what he was looking at.

It was the woman who had taken Thomas. She was standing in the doorway of the living room. Her hair skimmed the top of the timber doorframe because she was tall. And now that she could see her, Emily could smell her as well. She smelled strongly of some kind of musk. She smelled so exotic, foreign: she looked exotic and foreign, and so perfect. The woman calmly stepped into the hallway. She was aiming a small pistol at them.

"I'm sorry luv," Dot sobbed. "But she said she'd kill our Thomas if…"

Emily felt her head draining of any substance including her brain, until she felt her drained head might float off her shoulders and the rest of her body would just collapse on the floor in a heap. Her mind was jack-knifing. Thoughts were spinning and crashing around in her mind as though she were in a place devoid of sense, the sort of place only reserved for dreams, no, nightmares.

"'Ere what's goin' on? Put that gun down woman before yer do someone an injury," ordered PC Birkett, but the woman just laughed at him. Her laugh was remarkable, it was so musical, angelically so.

"This is going to be easier than I thought," she said still laughing. "I thought this little country of yours was supposed to harbour a sophisticated society and yet you produce a rotund village bobby the like of which I thought only existed in your folk tales. Still, all this backwardness falls in my favour," she said in her strange exotic accent.

"Whur's my brother?" Emily spat before PC Birkett was able to vent his rage.

"You will join him soon enough." Her voice was sinister.

"What d'yer want wi' us?" Emily snapped.

"All in good time my dear, all in good time." Iman's dark eyes glistened like cold wet stones.

"Is it 'cos I saw that stupid Hole? So what?" Emily snapped.

"Emily love," Dot said soothingly, she was trying to calm Emily down.

The woman's eyes narrowed as she looked from Emily to Dot and back again. Her lips curved into a thin unpractised smile.

"It's just a Hole! Yer can't do this ter us over a stupid, pointless Hole," and then because the woman was still smiling at her, and apparently enjoying her desperation, Emily added: "you… you… COW!"

Emily crashed to the floor. Iman Khan had slapped her cheek with full force.

"Em!" Dot screamed and crouched over her daughter's fallen body. "Shush Emily love, please shush. Don't say 'owt more. Yer'll get yersel inter more trouble luv."

Emily couldn't say anymore, she felt as though her jaw had been broken. Besides she knew she could only say worse things to the woman and she didn't want to get her mother into trouble as well.

"Get up. Both of you get up, NOW!" Iman was pointing the gun at them. Her fury was evident. With her spare hand she took the handcuffs from PC Birkett's belt. Then she handcuffed him and Dot together. Aiming her pistol at Emily's head she screamed at him: "Open the door!"

PC Birkett stood his ground. Iman pointed the gun at him instead. "Open the door I said," she ordered more calmly, but she was much more terrifying in her calmness. PC Birkett still did not move. Suddenly there was a terrific bang: it was the report of a gun. Dot screamed and hid her face in her hands. Emily's ears were ringing and she felt sick. PC Birkett was clutching his stomach. It was a few heart stopping moments before Emily realised that the woman had fired the bullet into the beam above PC Birkett's head. It was a warning shot. Unhurt but warned, PC Birkett reluctantly opened the door and they stepped outside into the cold winter night.

16

Jeremiah hugged himself into the wall more tightly when he heard the gun shot. Then he cautiously peered over the wall, anxiously watching as the man came out first, handcuffed to the girl's mother. The girl called Emily followed. He could see in her grim expression that she was afraid but trying her hardest to contain her fear. Then another woman appeared. She was the one with the gun, presumably the one who had fired the shot. For a brief moment Jeremiah's stomach knotted: he thought he recognised her just like he thought he recognised the girl earlier; but it was dark and the woman's face was corrupted by her snarl.

"Get a move on before I shoot you all right here. It is absolutely freezing out here," she hissed.

Her voice… Jeremiah's stomach tightened and painful spasms gripped him again. He'd heard that voice before. Iman Khan's video message came flooding back to him and he remembered her voice chiming the words: "*Once she is destroyed the 'Hole' will be all yours. The world will be yours my love: all yours!*" It was the same voice he could hear now snarling at these people. It was the voice of Iman Khan.

Jeremiah couldn't take his eyes off her. She was like a different person. The way she wielded the gun confidently, and the way she heartlessly stared at her captors, wasn't anything like the woman he thought he knew. He had known her as a warm, gentle woman, who came to his house smelling of all the sweet things in the world, so that he had thought she was an angel no less, he even... Jeremiah didn't want to admit to himself that he had been a little in love with her, not now, not after seeing her with that gun, not after his father had murdered him. She must have known what had happened. Looking at her now he could see that she wouldn't have cared, she was ruthless like his father. She carried that gun as though she really intended to use it, as though she'd used one many times before.

Jeremiah's stomach cramped again. To think he'd had a crush on a woman that couldn't care less if he lived or died. How stupid he had been, how naïve and stupid he was back then. The thought of his stupid, humiliating crush made him shudder. If only he had known then what he knew now, he wasn't stupid now: now he knew how to kill too.

Iman Khan suddenly seemed very close: too close. Jeremiah decided to hide in the small stone pigsty behind him until they had gone away. Turning on his hands and knees, Jeremiah's foot caught a loose stone near the base of the wall toppling over the stones above it. It made a terrible noise in the stillness of the night.

"What was that?" Iman hissed.

The clacking of loose stone as Iman Khan climbed over the wall to investigate almost made Jeremiah faint. He'd made it inside the dark pigsty but he was worried that he'd cornered himself. Iman's shadow suddenly emerged crouched in the open doorway of the sty. The moonlight shrouded her perfect female shape as she leaned in: one hand reaching out like a feeler; the other was waiving the gun into the dark corners. "Is there anyone there?" she said in a sweet voice as though she were kind. This woman, whose visits to his house had so often made him want to burst with happiness now made him too afraid to breathe. So Jeremiah held his breath, afraid that she would hear it and know that he was there. He realised his mistake too late. The air became pent up in his lungs. He was ready to explode. He would have to gasp and when he did, she would know he was there.

"Thur won't be any folk out 'ere on a night like this," the man called to her, "no one that don't 'ave business out this way any road."

Jeremiah prayed that she would heed the man's words, but she remained in the doorway as though she could sense him there, crouching in the dark corners. Jeremiah couldn't hold his breath any more. He really was going to faint. He had to gasp.

"Urgh!" Iman gasped simultaneously. She was waving something out of her face as she retreated out of the doorway. "Urgh, spiders," she gasped again with a shudder. She turned and momentarily looked back at the pigsty. She must have thought better of it because she climbed back over the wall towards her prisoners and ordered them to march away. Then she was gone. They were all gone.

Jeremiah didn't breathe a sigh of relief, or if he did he didn't remember, because he still felt afraid. She was gone but now his attention turned to that other thing. He could still feel something else around him, something lurking in the darkness, making him quiver with fear. He felt as though he was losing his mind, imagining someone creeping about in the shadows: in his shadow, breathing, as he hadn't dared to when the woman came looking for him.

Another bout of pain struck him in the stomach. It was excruciating pain deep within him, as though someone were crushing his intestines in a red hot vice. He doubled over gripping his stomach. The pain kept coming in waves, just as it had done when he'd lain in front of the dead sheep. He thought he was going to be sick again, until suddenly he felt hot, baking hot. His light-headedness got worse and he imagined he could see the shadow all of a sudden, and it was sneaking closer... closer... its hands were reaching for him...stifling him... suffocating him. Jeremiah threw up suddenly. His throat burned as he retched uncontrollably, emptying the pain onto the ground until he was left exhausted and shivering.

The fever began to abate, disappearing almost as

quickly as it had come, until it was replaced by the bitter cold again. Jeremiah was left badly shaken. He didn't know why he kept getting the pains or whether or not he was hallucinating when he saw that thing coming towards him. He breathed deeply to calm himself. When he felt able he crept out of the sty and peered out from behind the wall.

The figures in the distance were just approaching the brow of the hill. Once they were over, unless he followed, they would be gone. Jeremiah shivered, it was so cold, and the cottage looked so inviting. There might even be a fire or even dry clothes. He watched the figures begin to shorten and then disappear over the hill. He should follow them, help the girl, but first he must help himself. He would search the cottage and worry about finding them again later.

17

*A*n old rickety window around the side of the cottage seemed like as good a place as any to break in. The crooked metal frame was loose; even so it only opened a little before becoming stuck. Jeremiah pushed hard. The window opened with a sudden jolt and the latch swung away knocking a vase and a photograph off the window ledge. Jeremiah ducked down, hiding in case anyone came to investigate the disturbance. Nobody did. The coast was clear so he climbed in the window.

The glass from the photo frame crunched beneath his feet. Jeremiah picked up the photograph that had been inside the frame. He recognised two of the people in the picture immediately: the girl and the woman who had opened the door to let her in. He assumed that she was the girl's mother. There was also a man and a boy in the picture. Jeremiah read the caption underneath. "*Thomas and Emily at me mum's 85th.*" Jeremiah studied the girl's face. He was sure he'd seen her face before. He shrugged dismissively; he often thought he recognised strangers from somewhere. More often than not the familiarity of such strangers never amounted to anything more than coincidence. Jeremiah propped the frameless picture back on the windowsill and brushing past the Christmas tree, headed for the door. He shuddered as he felt the shadow pass in front of him.

The stairs were creaky and uneven, the wallpaper old and flowery, nothing like anything Jeremiah had ever seen before, except perhaps in old story books, or black and white films. As soon as he was at the top of the stairs, Jeremiah began checking rooms. He checked three rooms, the main bedroom, a box room, and the bathroom. He was surprised to find the fourth room hers, Emily's. He didn't know why it surprised him. He knew it was hers though because of the rosy patchwork quilt that lay in a puddle on the floor, only one of its corners still clinging to the bed; and there was a dish on top of the dresser with things in it. He didn't know what the things were other than trinkets for girls but it was a mark of her, a mark of Emily. Jeremiah scooped some trinkets into his fingers. They made her seem more real: less forgettable. Jeremiah pushed the guilt from his mind and threw the trinkets back into the dish. He would find her. He would help her. Just not right now, not until he felt stronger, not until he felt ready.

Lying next to the trinkets was a notepad. Jeremiah picked it up and flicked through it. He wondered who Damien was. Whoever he was she loved him ninety nine percent. She was good at drawing he noticed. Her endless sketches of horses' heads were brilliant; but it wasn't the horse's heads or the repeatedly scribbled name Damien that kept catching his attention, it was the black circles. Big ones, small ones, ones with strange unclear edges; but all filled with as much utter blackness as her biro could muster, so that she had gone through the paper trying to give a depth to the black ink that the paper just couldn't take. They were Holes: black Holes. Jeremiah placed the notebook back down, ignored the brass mirror and turned to see the shadow dart across the door.

There had been mirrors in all four previous rooms and on the landing. It was only now as he held the doorknob of the last room that Jeremiah realised he had subconsciously been avoiding looking at them. He had been afraid of what he might see; afraid that he would see a dead person's pallor, or the crooked shoulder and broken neck that Shae-nae had described. He didn't want to see himself like that. He felt alive in this cold place and he didn't want to spoil the feeling. But as he opened the door to the last room and saw the big mirror on the wardrobe door, his curiosity began to get the better of him.

It was a boy's room, the boy in the photograph perhaps? The bed was unmade as though it had only recently been slept in, and some recently dated comics made the boy current, alive. Where was he then? And where for that matter was the father? Why did he not come to their aid when the girl and her mother were being taken hostage? Jeremiah touched the boy's things: his guitar; the

127

well-read SAS survival book, and the broken binoculars. *Thomas...* Jeremiah remembered the caption in the picture. The boy's name was Thomas. His clothes lay discarded on the floor. Jeremiah picked them up. They were old, threadbare and cheap but they were dry. He quickly put them on and immediately felt better to be out of the cold damp clothes that had been clinging to him.

Pulling back the curtain a fraction Jeremiah peered out over the snow covered landscape. Somewhere out there was that girl Emily and maybe her brother too. This cottage was their home. In so many ways Jeremiah felt as though he was still in that place, or in some terrible dream, but there were other things that were so real. Jeremiah glanced down at the window ledge... like this pile of books, he thought. He picked one of them up. It was a book about oil. It reminded Jeremiah of his father. Then he noticed the other books. They were strange books for a boy that looked about the same age as himself: books about Iraq and the ancient city of Babylonia; books about archaeology and the Holy Grail; and more books about oil.

A stack of newspapers lay on the floor next to a scrapbook. The scrapbook was obviously a work in progress: the glue, scissors and scraps of old newspaper lay around untidily. Jeremiah picked the scrap book up and flicked through it. A picture of his father jumped out of the page at him. He sucked in his breath. It was the first time he'd seen his father since his death. During that time, however long it had been, his father's face had become less and less clear, until it had become little more than a gold tooth in a dark mysterious face. But here he was again in this picture, as clear as a bell. Jeremiah could even see the small white scar on his chin, a mark of his childhood when the handle bars of his bike had twisted and smashed through his chin during an accident. You couldn't see his most striking scar though, the one that few knew about, the one that Jeremiah knew about because his scar was the same.

Under the picture was some handwritten scrawl. The boy's untidy handwriting said:

Levi Washington. The man what chased us down by the lake. What is he doing here?

What was that supposed to mean? Why on earth would his father chase this boy? Jeremiah felt sick suddenly. His father had chased him and it had resulted in his murder. Where was the boy? There was no sign of him. Maybe he too was murdered. Jeremiah suddenly felt the need to find out where he was and why his father was here too. It didn't feel like a place he knew. It didn't even feel like the states because the accents were so difficult to understand at times. He understood enough to establish at least that they were speaking some kind of English. Jeremiah picked up a book called 'Darkmere'. The book had a beautiful picture of a tranquil moonlit lake on its cover. It might be a library book, he thought, they all looked like the sort of books you'd pick up in a library. He flipped over its cover and looked inside. He was right, a stamp on the inside cover suddenly had his interest. The stamp said: *Darkmere public library, Old Courthouse, Darkmere, Cumbria.* Curious, he thought, that the place stamped inside had the same name as the cover.

Jeremiah ran his finger down the index to see if any of the chapter headings jumped out at him. The first chapter did, it was headed: *How Darkmere got its name.* Jeremiah scanned the first paragraph. It seemed the subject of Darkmere's name was a constant source of speculation in the village. All sorts of myths and horror stories were associated with it, but the fact of the matter was that there were an unusually high number of drownings in Darkmere, and this fact alone gave credence to the number one theory of how Darkmere got its name.

Suddenly a thought occurred to Jeremiah. He quickly crossed the room to the boy's desk. On it was a cheap plastic globe. He found the small unconvincingly shaped, green mound that represented England. It was difficult to read, England was so small, but there it was, written in the north west of the green mound, a county called Cumbria and underneath in Italics it said: *The Lake District.* He was not in that place, he should have known as soon as he saw Iman. He was in England and so it would seem was his father.

Suddenly everything started flooding back to him: the queue, the light, the sprite taking his hand and leading him… yes, the light, he knew it would give him life. He'd said so to Shae-nae. The light was a ticket out of that place, a ticket back from death, an open door that took them back into the living world; and here he was back in the living world, in England of all places. Jeremiah suddenly sobered; he was in England but he was close to danger and it all felt so much like that place that he was unable to feel exhilarated. Instead he slumped onto the bed. 'I must be alive then,' he whispered and a faint trace of a smile dared to cross his lips. 'I'm in England, not that place… England.' But the smile was only transient. 'What the hell am I doing in England anyway?'

Suddenly Jeremiah sat bolt upright. In the E-mail, Iman had told his father to go to England, the place where the Hole was. The Hole, wasn't it the cause of his murder? The fact that he'd read something about it on his father's computer, something he didn't even understand, had driven his father to have him murdered. They were all here because of the Hole. What was it about this goddamn Hole?

Jeremiah wasn't thinking about the Hole though when he shuddered, he was thinking about his father again. His father was close. At first the notion that he might see his father again frightened him, but as it sunk in he hoped it would be true. He hoped he would see his father again, and he hoped his father would see him. He wanted to see the look on his father's face when the son he murdered stood before him alive, and with all the revenge in the world gleaming in his eyes.

His fantasy came to an abrupt end when he suddenly became flushed with doubt. What if this feeling of being alive in England, and so close to his father was just some dead person's delusion? What if he were in that place still and this was all a dream? There was one way to find out. Jeremiah climbed off the bed and stood up. He closed his eyes and blindly positioned himself in front of the full-length mirror on the wardrobe door. He'd been avoiding the mirrors in the other rooms. He hadn't wanted to stare his own death in the face and see his own grey corpse mouldering and festering before his very eyes; or see his dead pallor, or see the crooked shoulder and broken neck that he suspected would be there. But now the time had come: the time had come to face the truth. He only had to open his eyes and he would see. Jeremiah trembled. There was doubt. He sucked in his breath. He would overcome his doubt. He would listen to his instincts and his instincts told him he was alive. He composed himself. When I open my eyes, he thought, I will know once and for all.

Heart pounding, Jeremiah opened his eyes. The fear did not grip him straightaway because he thought he must have been imagining it. The crooked shoulder, the grey skin, the broken neck; none of the things he had been expecting to see of himself were visible. He looked normal and a wave of relief washed over him. But his initial relief turned to terror. He swayed and clutched the bedpost as he watched the shadow pass close behind him in the mirror and then rise up tall behind him, its mouth agape, bloody and muddy fingers grasping and coming down over him, trying to engulf him. It was no longer a shadow. It looked like a dead kid: a distorted dead kid, all grey skin and crooked bones, broken by violence, by murder. It looked as he thought he would have looked: its hair was the same except matted with blood; its clothes the same but they were also covered in mud and blood, and also grass stains. But the dead kid was all wrong. He was all distorted and elongated, and grey and slimy. It was totally repulsive, *and the smell...* It couldn't be a dead boy surely? It couldn't be himself dead. It must be a creature from that place. It was a sprite, his sprite, cruelly mimicking him. If he was alive then why was this hellish creature shadowing him? Jeremiah's hope was crushed.

When Jeremiah turned from the mirror the sprite had gone. Although he could not see it anymore he knew it was still there, he could feel its presence, a presence he desperately wanted to escape from. Forgetting his weapon, Jeremiah leapt off the bed and ran. He wanted to leave the cottage and run forever in the opposite direction. He bolted down the crooked stairs stumbling at the bottom and slamming painfully into the front door. The door was locked. A stiff old-fashioned bolt at the top stood between him and freedom. Jeremiah reached up for the bolt. His fingers burned as he tried to pull it free but it was stuck fast. His escape was taking too long. The hairs on the back of his neck stood on end. He could feel the sprite coming for him. At last the bolt came free. Jeremiah felt a temporary sense of relief. He turned to see the shadow moving across the landing. It came to the top of the stairs and hovered. Jeremiah knew it was staring at him even though its eyes were in shadow. Turning back to the door he began fumbling at the latch, but the door still wouldn't open, it was jarring against something else. The fear and frustration inside Jeremiah was reaching fever pitch and he could not think straight. He didn't notice another thick old bolt at the foot of the door that needed opening.

The shadow was sneaking down the stairs now, as though it were sliding on its belly.

"Open you son of a bitch… please open!" Jeremiah cried out as he desperately rattled the door, but it still would not open and the sprite kept sliding closer until it was close enough to touch him. It reached out towards him. Jeremiah cried out again and recoiled from its shadowy feelers. Letting go of the door, he ducked under the feelers and doubled back along the hallway, panting and gasping.

The shadow came after him into the dark room. Jeremiah couldn't see it now but he knew it had followed him. He slumped onto a chair feeling defeated. "Go away," he yelled, pummelling the table in front of him with his fists. "Go away, you goddamned freak!" He was thinking of the image he'd seen in the mirror: the image of the walking dead, the hideousness of its rotting corpse. But it wasn't just any old rotting corpse it was his rotting corpse and it was following him around, reminding him that he was dead, murdered and stinking of rotten flesh. If only he could get some space from it, that thing, that grotesque other world albatross, he needed space to think. He knew he wasn't going to get space from it though. He began to understand that the sprite was a part of him, part of his death anyway. Jeremiah looked up at the doorway where the shadow was skulking about and sobbed again. "What do you want from me? Why do you keep following me?" He didn't expect an answer and he didn't get one.

18

Sudden pains gripped Jeremiah's stomach again. But they were not like the ones he'd felt in the pigsty, or back in the snow where the sheep lay dying. He hadn't felt one of these pains for a good while. Even in the castle he'd been well fed. Now though, he realised he'd lost count of the hours or days that might have passed since he'd last eaten anything. It was odd that even during death he should feel real hunger. When he was alive, he'd assumed that if there were an afterlife, it would automatically free him from such mortal constraints as pain, hunger and thirst. But his afterlife so far was proving wrong all his mortal assumptions; and most confusing of all was that the desire to survive was as great, if not greater in death.

His stomach cramped again. It was the smell. He was surrounded by food, masses of it. He was in a kitchen. The table was laden but everything looked grey and unappetising in the dark kitchen, where the only form of light was moonlight streaming in a generous window that ran almost the length of one wall. Grey or not, it was food and it didn't smell off. Jeremiah's juices flowed. He picked up a small round pie and held it up to his nose inhaling deeply. The smell of the butter pastry and the sweet cinnamon filling made the painful knot in his stomach tighten and he began to salivate. He wanted to cram the pie in his mouth whole, but something stopped him. It was probably drugged, just like everything else. In defiance, he threw the pie at the wall, watching its dark innards splatter. He wouldn't obey his instincts this time. He wasn't ready to succumb to another deep slumber. Waking up to find himself still here, in this place, would just be too terrible to bear. In the castle the despair had always been at its worst when he had just woken. He decided it was best not to sleep at all.

If only he could find Shae-nae. He needed her now. He missed her. How odd, he thought, that he should miss someone he met only briefly when he was dead. The coarseness that had bothered him initially didn't matter now. She was more like him than anyone. She was the only human he'd met who shared his terrifying experience. She too had a sprite following her, feeding her drugged things and keeping her prisoner; she understood. Jeremiah shuddered and felt the shadowy sprite sneak closer. She could be anywhere. He might never see her again. He wondered if their meeting had been but a brief encounter, another glimmer of hope crushed when the light ripped her away from him. Had she ever even existed outside his nightmares?

Suddenly a loud rattling noise behind him distracted him from his solemn thoughts. Jeremiah turned quickly but could see nothing behind the plastic screen where the noise was coming from. The rattling became frantic. He scanned the room for the sprite but he could not see it, or its shadow. It must be behind the screen making the noise, he concluded, unless it was one of those creatures, like the ones in the queue. So he scanned the room for a place to hide and spotted the dark recess of a larder by the window. With his heart thudding he ran for cover, squeezing himself in between the tins and cereal packets. He was only partially hidden but it was the best he could do.

The rattling stopped suddenly. There was the sound of a creaky hinge and then the plastic screen crashed forward into the room. Jeremiah squeezed himself up against the shelves, his eyes were half closed, his face half turned away. He could see it. It was coming into the room. It wasn't a creature, or even the sprite. It was something else altogether: something he wasn't expecting at all.

19

*E*mily was standing in the back doorway. She was panting heavily and her eyes were wide open so that she had the look of a wild beast about her. She was hesitant, as though she didn't know what to do. Then, quite suddenly, she decided to run across the room, yank open a drawer and pull out a long sharp kitchen knife. She wielded the kitchen knife as if to prove to herself that she could, and would use it.

At least she wasn't one of those ugly creatures, or a sprite. Jeremiah really wanted to befriend her but the knife and the wildness about her made him shrink back into the cupboard. Instead, silent and still, he watched her movements for sometime; that is, until he became aware of a broom handle sticking in his ribs. He tried to ignore it at first. He was hoping the girl would go soon enough and he would move unnoticed then. But Emily didn't go because she didn't really know what she was doing. All the while the pain in Jeremiah's ribs was becoming more and more unbearable, as though the handle had pierced his skin and was threatening to break through his rib bones.

She was taking too long. She had no direction. She was

randomly pulling things out of cupboards. Jeremiah couldn't wait. He would have to shift, just a little. She wouldn't notice because she was so absorbed in her frantic task, besides he could stand it no longer. A little bead of sweat broke out on his forehead as he moved slowly, carefully... But it was no good, his elbow caught on an open packet of spaghetti. The loose spaghetti fell to the floor like rain.

Emily wheeled around with the knife in her hand.

"Who the..."

She was looking in his direction. Her eyes were adjusting to the dark. She would see him. Jeremiah stepped out of the cupboard and threw his hands up in the air in a gesture of surrender. "It's okay," he said. "Don't be afraid. I'm not one of them. I saw that woman with the gun taking you hostage. I'm on your side, I promise."

She stood back afraid. Her knife was poised. "Stay back," she hissed savagely waving the knife at him. "Yer one of 'em I can tell. Yer don't fool me. Yer like that man," she said fearfully.

"What man. I'm not like any man. I'm here alone," protested Jeremiah.

It was not going well. He could see that she was terrified enough to use the knife. He knew, he'd been that terrified before, in the castle and in the queue: particularly in the queue. Such terror could push her over the edge as it had done to him.

"See, yer an American an' all. Yer must think I wur born

yest'day. I swur," she gestured with the knife again, "one false move an' I'll kill yer." Then she pulled out another drawer. With her eyes still trained on Jeremiah she blindly rummaged inside it. Eventually, Emily pulled out a ball of string.

"Ah, come on, don't tie me up. We might be able to help each other."

"Shut it. I'm sick o' lot o' yer. I don't know what yer up ter but I'm sick of it. I'm gonna tie yer up and use yer ter get me brother back. I'll kill yer like a rat if I 'ave ter so watch it. Now sit down on that chur."

Prodding him in the back with the tip of the knife, Emily made Jeremiah sit on a chair while she began to bind his hands tightly behind his back, and the back of the chair, with the thin nylon string.

"Hey, that's too tight. It's burning. Ah, it's cutting into my arms!"

"Shut it, I said," she snarled, pushing the tip of the knife, into his back again. "Don't even so much as wriggle yer little toes in yer boots or thur'll be trouble. One false move an' I'll cut yer tongue out just fer starters."

Jeremiah did as he was told but he couldn't stop the shadow moving. It came beside him. Involuntarily, he shivered. Emily rounded on him, wielding the knife warningly. "What wur that?" she hissed jumpily.

"Nothing, it was nothing." Jeremiah pleaded.

"I saw summat movin' out the corner o' me eye. I'm not stupid."

"I was shivering from the cold that's all. I'm not used to it. Sorry." She'd definitely kill him if he tried to explain about the sprite; she was way too freaked out.

Her eyes were narrowed with suspicion and she was looking him up and down. At length she said: "Aye, bloody cold is right. Well yer better get used ter it." Then she said no more while she tested the weight of two carrier bags that she had been cramming with food. She wasn't satisfied because she shook her head and disappeared outside the back door where there was a porch. She returned with a military style backpack. She reloaded the food into it with some matches, a torch, a small, useless first aid kit, and the rest of the string. She held onto the large kitchen knife.

"Are you running away or something?"

"I'm gonna get me bruther and me mum back and then all three us are gonna' run away. You and your kind will never find us again." Then choked, she added: "That's if they 'aven't hurt 'em already."

"What do you mean me and my kind?" Did she think he was one of those creatures, did he look like the rotting corpse of a boy to her?

"Shut it! Yer knaw what I mean," she said. Her face was contorted by fear and rage and as though she really wanted to kill him, she jabbed the knife under his nose. Jeremiah threw his head back to avoid the blade. He lost his balance and the chair fell backwards causing him to

142

whack his leg on the underside of the table as he fell. A sharp pin underneath snagged his flesh leaving a burning gash.

"Jesus Christ! You're crazy. Ah! My leg!" he cried out. He wanted to clutch his leg, nurse the pain, but his arms were tied behind his back being crushed underneath his own weight and the weight of the chair. Even in the darkness he could see that his trousers were ripped and the dark patch was blood.

Emily came closer to look at his leg. Her face didn't look as angry as it had been, as though she felt a flicker of remorse. She dampened some kitchen paper with water and cleaned off the blood before wrapping a kitchen towel around his leg.

"Never mind my leg, it's my arms, my arms," he gasped.

Emily tipped the chair back up.

"I caught my leg on a nail or something. It's sticking out under the table," he gasped.

It wasn't a nail. Emily could see that it was a pin of some kind. She looked at it cautiously. She'd never seen it before, never known it was there before, but then she couldn't remember having a reason to look at the underside of the kitchen table before. Emily pressed the tip of the pin carefully. It had some give as though attached to a spring. She bent down to look at it more closely. She couldn't make out what the pin was for in the darkness.

Her curiosity got the better of her though, and she pressed it firmly so that it clicked. Something hard shot out and hit her in the side of the face; it was the same side that the woman had hit her on. Emily fell backwards. The pain was blinding.

"You okay?" Jeremiah asked.

"'Course," she replied through gritted teeth. When she was able, she looked up at the thing that had struck her. It was a drawer, and now it was open.

Emily reached inside the drawer and pulled out a slim black leather file. The file was quite plain but for an even blacker circle on the front cover and some extraordinary gold writing, which said:

Translations of the Babylonia 6X
scriptures and prophesy

The words were written in some sort of gold leaf, although each letter shone in the moonlight as though it had been written in something more special.

"I've never seen 'owt like this before," Emily said to herself. Jeremiah hadn't either.

Emily pulled a small maglite out of her back pack. She clicked it on and directed the light over the documents inside. They were photographs of ancient text but she didn't recognise any of the letters or symbols, let alone understand the meaning. There were also sketches scribbled onto scraps of paper, as though someone had been making notes on the strange text. Whoever it was made reference to constellations, tides, and pertinent dates including Christmas Day, but none of it meant anything to her.

"What does this stuff mean?" Emily waved the pages under Jeremiah's nose, directing the beam of light into his eyes.

Jeremiah clamped his eyelids shut. "I don't know, I honestly don't know. I told you I'm on your side," he said, although now he was not so sure.

She looked back at the papers and flicked through them again. Suddenly she felt the blood drain from her head. Christmas day, she thought. "It's Christmas day now," she said to herself. This period in time was significant. This dark Christmas night was significant. It was why the strangers were here, all edgy and dangerous. Frustrated by her partial understanding she flicked through the rest of the document quickly, but apart from a few dull portraits there was nothing else of any significance: nothing that she understood anyway. She decided to keep the file. When she had escaped with Thomas and her mother she would go to London. Someone there would be able to translate it. Maybe the people at Scotland Yard would know what to do with it.

Something else slid out from between the booklet's covers as she tried to put it into her bag. It was a slim paper file. "*Directory of UK Kinsmen, Loyal worshipers of the Hole,*" was written on the front in the same shimmering gold leaf. Emily picked up the file and opened it. It was a register of names. The list of names was endless. They were categorised by county and then subdivided by postcode. Each had a contact mobile phone number. There were thousands of them, 637843 to be precise. They must be everywhere these worshippers of *that* Hole she worried, like some kind of cult.

Some of the so-called 'Kinsmen' and women were pictured. Emily scanned the pictures. She decided to keep the list as well so she would know who to trust in future when she escaped with Thomas and her mother. She didn't know about the boy though. He was an American. He wasn't on this list. There must be another list for Americans.

"What is it?" asked Jeremiah, "What have you found?"

"Don't act the innocent wi' me," she hissed as she continued scanning the pictures. Jeremiah could tell it was something significant because she hadn't said a word or stopped frowning since she'd picked the file up.

Emily noticed that the Kinsmen or women that were pictured were referred to as 'High Kinsmen' and 'High Kinswomen'. She guessed that meant they had some special significance. She was shocked to see that she recognised two of the faces from the television: one was an actor from her mum's favourite soap, 'Coronation Street', another was a children's television presenter. Then a picture shocked her so much that she felt as though she couldn't breathe.

146

Emily stumbled backwards dropping the booklet and the torch on the floor. She turned and buried her face into her arms sobbing aloud as though she had forgotten anyone else was in the room.

Jeremiah leaned over the booklet. The torch beam skimmed over the picture that had upset her. He recognised the face. It had the same stern but proud expression he'd seen in the picture that he'd knocked over. It was her father. The caption beneath his picture said:

24312/ Master Tanimesh Tianan
Currently known as High Kinsmen Bill Hayward
Gifted reader and translator of ancient Galadric Scriptures
Mobile: 07770914230

Jeremiah looked up at Emily hunched over the kitchen work surface. Even in the darkness he could see her shoulders shaking as she sobbed. He felt bad for her even though she had tied him up. "You didn't know about your father, huh?" he said softly.

After a while she sniffed: "What d'yer care any road?"

"I'm sorry," Jeremiah added. He didn't know what else to say.

Emily sniffed again: "It ses he wur responsible fer workin' out thur wur summat in Iraq. It ses…" she picked the file and the torch up again and read the smaller print underneath her father's picture, "'*…his great gifts lead to*

147

the discovery of the Babylonia site 6X and the translation of the scriptures found therein.' Whatever that means, but I guess it has summat ter do wi' all that stuff on't news. No wonder 'e wur so obsessed by it. You'd know all about it though wouldn't yer, seein' as yer a part of all this?"

"Say that again." Jeremiah asked ignoring her accusation. "Say it again, you know the bit about Babylonia."

His question diffused her anger. "'*...his great gifts,'*" she said again, "'*lead to the discovery of the Babylonia site 6X and the translation of the scriptures found therein.'*"

"Babylonia 6X? I heard all about that on my father's computer. I think my father is a Kinsman too whatever that means. It seems our fathers are in this together." Jeremiah watched the girl's eyes narrow. She wasn't buying it.

"What else did yer hear about? Yer seem ter know an awful lot about these folk fer someone who's claimin' to be a victim in all this."

But Jeremiah wasn't listening. He was trying to piece together what he remembered of Iman's video message. "That woman, the one that was holding you hostage earlier, she's called Iman Khan and she sent my father a video message. She was in some sort of cave in Iraq. I think the cave was the 6X site. There were ancient paintings and writings on the walls of the cave that looked like those," he nodded at the photocopies in her hand, "but none of it meant anything to me. She did say something about a Hole coming for someone and once she, whoever *she* is, is destroyed the world would be all his, you know, all my father's."

"A Hole? What sort o' Hole?"

"I dunno'. She didn't say anything else about it. There was a picture of a Hole in one of the paintings on the wall, but it didn't look like anything special." Jeremiah suddenly seemed to go into a state of shock.

"What is it? What else did she say?"

He shook his head as though he was just coming to from a faint. "I don't understand it, I just know it's bad," he said.

"What is fer God's sake?"

"It's you!"

"What is, what yer talkin' about?"

There was a picture of a lake and a mountain on the wall of the cave. There was a girl standing between the lake and mountain. That girl looked exactly like you."

"What?"

"I knew I recognised you from somewhere."

Emily was silent for a while. She needed to process what he was saying.

"Don't be daft," she said eventually, "how would anyone in Iraq know me? It's just a coincidence."

Jeremiah continued: "She said the Hole would be all his. Her exact words were: 'Once *she* is destroyed the 'Hole' will be all yours.'"

"What did she mean once *she* is destroyed the world

will be all his? Who's she? *Me* d'yer mean? What the 'ell are yer tryin' ter say? Yer tryin' ter turn this round and make out I'm the baddy. I'm not stupid yer knaw. I can see what yer up ter."

Emily was shaking, she was furious and scared. She picked up the knife thinking she should shut him up once and for all, but threatening him wouldn't suddenly make what he was saying untrue. She kept visualising the Hole and the mesmeric blackness that she'd seen inside it. She understood the moment she had her first glimpse of it that there was a power in it that would be desired by men. Now she was terrified that somehow she was a part of it too.

Jeremiah realised he needed to back off about the cave painting; he didn't want to risk frightening her any more.

"Do you ever wonder why this place is called Darkmere?" he asked, hoping to diffuse her anger and divert attention.

"I don't, but everyone's bin goin' on 'bout it again since the family o' tourists went missin'. Fer me though the reason is simple, it's 'cos o' Scar Fell. Rain or shine, summer or winter, that mountain casts a dark shadow o'er the lake mekkin' water look black. That's why it's called Darkmere and fer no other reason than that."

"I saw a book upstairs, it said there were a lot of drownings in the lake, you know, more than normal. I mean considering the circumstances don't you think there may be some significance?"

"No I don't. It's now't more than a coincidence. If this town wur called Happy Valley same folk would still be 'ere interferin wi' us lives. That Levi Washington fella's behind it all. They might as well call 'im the President o' the United States fer all't power 'es got. He chased our Thomas down by't lake."

Jeremiah's stomach knotted again at the mention of his father's name and he remembered the boy's notes in his scrapbook. He wondered how long he'd been dead. He was trying to remember the day he was killed. It was September he was sure. It had been a beautiful day, followed by a balmy evening: an evening that would be his last. It was Christmas in Darkmere.

"I've been dead for months."

"What?"

"Nothing. Sorry."

"D'yer reckon it could be about oil then? Thomas and I thought all this stuff, the Hole and everythin', might be about Oil and that the rest is just hocus pocus, designed to put other oil prospectors off the scent," said Emily hopefully. That explanation would be best, she thought.

"Could be, I suppose." It would explain a lot, thought Jeremiah, possibly even why his father had killed him. If his father had found a new oil field he wouldn't want anyone blowing it, not least his own son, there would be too much riding on it.

Jeremiah's train of thought was interrupted. Emily was sobbing. He would have put an arm around her if he hadn't been tied up. Instead he spoke softly to her. "My father betrayed me too. He..." Jeremiah didn't know how to explain. He knew he couldn't tell her that his father had killed him, then he'd have to explain why he wasn't in a coffin and she'd totally freak out if he tried to explain that.

"He what?" she prompted him.

"He tried to hurt me. He saw me watching the confidential video message I was telling you about and he tried to hurt me to shut me up."

"What happened?"

"I escaped. I just ran away. I've come to hate the man that I looked up to more than anyone in the world. I've come to hate the man that I..." Jeremiah's voice tailed off, he couldn't say the word 'loved,' it was too painful. He gritted his teeth and tried not to sob. He could tell that she hadn't made the connection yet, that Levi Washington was his father. He guessed it was too big a connection and she just had too much other stuff going on in her head; but he wanted her to guess, he wanted to tell her everything about his murder, the castle, the loneliness of death but he couldn't, he knew the full story sounded too surreal.

"I wish I could bring mesell'ter believe yer," she said. Her voice was muffled because her face was still resting on her arms.

"You can believe me but I don't know how to convince you. If I told you all I know, all that's happened to me, you really wouldn't believe me. I know if I heard my story from a complete stranger I would think they were crazy."

"Are yer?"

"Am I what?"

Emily lifted her face. Her eyes locked with his. "Crazy?" she asked, noticing how his face looked knowing beyond its years. It was almost the face of a man.

Jeremiah did not answer. He didn't know the answer. He hadn't considered that he might be crazy. What if the whole experience had been the result of some sort of schizophrenic episode? His experiences felt real, but isn't that what all schizo's think? Now faced with an opportunity to explain himself he felt silly, realising how preposterous it would sound. It was impossible for anyone to believe his story, except Shae-nae, if only he knew where she was.

Jeremiah's silence deepened Emily's suspicion. She stood up and began shoving the glossy booklet back into a pocket on the inside of the file, but the booklet wouldn't go back in, it was crumpling up another piece of paper inside. Using two fingers she pulled out a single piece of crumpled photographic paper. She flattened it out. The torchlight was dimming but the light was just about sufficient. Emily shone it on the paper. It was a picture: a very detailed picture, so detailed and intricate that at first she couldn't make out what exactly the picture was depicting. The torch flickered and went out. "Damn it," she cursed. She needed more light. She took the picture to the window and examined it in the bright moonlight. The detail seemed to knit together all at once, making perfect sense in a sudden flourish.

"Argh!"

Emily dropped the picture as though it had burned her hands.

"What is it?" asked Jeremiah.

Reluctantly, Emily picked it up again, holding it between her very fingertips as if to avoid contamination from the horrible image that it portrayed. Suppressing her instinct to recoil she looked at the ghastly image again. She was looking at a photocopy of an old etching. It was entitled: '*The feeding of the Hole*'.

It looked like a human landfill site. Great mounds of contorted bodies, like great mounds of rubbish, were being tipped into a Hole from the back of hundreds of carts, all queuing to take their turn to deposit their load. Some of the bodies were still alive and were locked together in last desperate embraces, there were even children and babies…Emily closed her eyes. It was the terrified expressions on their faces, a baby's face in particular, that stuck in her brain. Vultures circled above. Bodies, too many to number were piled into the dark reaches of the Hole from all sides while beams of light shot up out from the depths, reaching for the stars, as though the bodies were exciting something deep within the Hole, giving it life in exchange for death.

"Armageddon," Emily gasped.

"What is it? What have you found?" asked Jeremiah.

Emily's knees were trembling. She could barely cross the room back to him. Her hands shook as she tried to light the Christmas candle on the table. It took five attempts before it was lit. Emily pushed the light and the picture towards him. The light flickered over the picture and she watched the change come over his face.

Jeremiah recoiled, horrified, "I'm not a part of this," he gasped.

Emily picked up the candle and held it to his face. She didn't know whether to set him on fire or cut him loose. She hadn't doubted his expression of genuine horror when he'd looked at the picture though.

"What does it mean?" she asked looking at the hideous details again despite herself. The people were dehumanised. They were nothing but fodder for the Hole. Some were broken, with contorted limbs thrust out at angles unnatural to the human form; and their faces... their faces were gripped by a fear of something far greater than any pain they might be feeling. As Emily studied the picture more closely she realised that the shafts of light coming out of the Hole were more than that, they had form. Each shaft looked like a grotesquely elongated hand with fingers as long to match. There were hundreds of them reaching up for the bodies and wrapping their long illuminated fingers around limbs and hair, cruelly and facelessly snatching the bodies from their lives on earth and pulling them down into the deep, dark, depths of the infinite Hole.

Fear for her brother washed over Emily anew. "They've taken me brother. Me own father took 'im because I looked down a Hole. I think it wur this Hole, the one they've all bin lookin' fer. My God what 'ave I done?"

"Wait a minute you've seen the Hole? Why the hell didn't you say so before?" Jeremiah was incredulous.

"I thought I 'ad said. I mean, I don't knaw."

"When? When did you see it?"

"Yest'day. That's what started all this business. They left us alone before I looked at it. I didn't know it would be such a big deal. I mean, at worst I thought if I got caught I'd get a police caution for trespass, yer know first offence an' all. Me brother got one once fer throwin' stones at an old power station and smashin't windows. I figured just lookin' behind thur tarpaulin wurn't even as bad as that."

Jeremiah was reeling. The girl had seen the Hole. He could barely contain his fear and excitement. "So what did it look like?"

"Well, like I said to our Thomas, it wur black, but black like I never seen before: blacker 'n nature. It didn't 'ave a bottom either, well not so yer could see any road, and I dropped a stone down it and heard nowt, no splashin' like, or 'owt like that. And the lake, well it wur weird, it just sort o' swirled around the outside of it, as though some sort o' invisible force were 'oldin' it all back. It made the hurs on't

156

back o' me neck stand up I'm tellin' yer." Emily shuddered. "And now when I look at this picture and think what's happened since…" she bit her lip and swallowed to stop herself crying.

Jeremiah was only half listening. His mind was whirring. He was remembering the endless black sketches on her dresser. A Hole like the one she was describing was unnatural. Coming back to life was unnatural wasn't it? Were the two things connected? Where did the light come from and where was it going? What if the light somehow spat him out here via the Hole, what if it spat out his sprite too? After everything he'd been through, surely anything was possible. Then he remembered something else he'd seen on his father's computer screen; something about predicted sales of… what were they called? HSPBs or Heaven Sent Perpetuity Bonds. Whatever they were, they didn't sound like they had much to do with oil. He looked at the etching again, it bore no resemblance to his idea of Heaven but it bore a horrific resemblance to his idea of Hell. Weren't Heaven and Hell connected somehow, like love and hate, life and death? You can't have one without the other and all that. Surely if you can go down a Hole you can come back up out if it, that's the nature of a Hole isn't it?

Emily interrupted his thoughts. "I know thur's summat terrible about it. That's why these folk are protectin' their interest in it wi' guns and stuff. Powerful folk like. That Levi fella is right powerful, he looks like a movie star, no more like a hip-hop star or summat. I never sin no one like him round this way before. That's what I wur sayin' 'bout you. I thought you were like 'im, yer know related or summat. Mind, now I can see yer not. He's rich, summat tells us you're not." She looked at his dirty ripped clothes and his soiled face.

"I am."

"Yer what, rich?"

"Related to him." Jeremiah's heart skipped a beat as he said it. He was taking a huge risk.

It took Emily a few seconds to understand what he was trying to tell her. "I knew it," she said. Then she rolled her eyes and slapped her head as though she was punishing herself for being stupid. "He's yer father. Fer God's sake I shudda' sin it comin'" Emily shoved the etching into her backpack and slung it over her shoulder: "I should kill yer so yer can't tell 'em 'owt about me when they come back lookin', but I can't bring mesell ter. All I can say is this, yer better 'ope they do come back lookin' or else yer gonna' rot right thur on that chur." Emily made for the back door.

"Wait," Jeremiah called. "Wait. Hear me out. Didn't your father just betray you? Isn't it possible then that my father betrayed me?"

Emily stopped in the doorway, her back still to him. "Go on," she hissed impatiently. "I'm waitin'."

Jeremiah swallowed. His tongue felt thick, he didn't

know how to begin. It was difficult when she wouldn't even look at him.

"Remember what I was saying about that e-mail to my father, well there was something else."

"Like what?"

"Stuff about HSPBs."

Emily turned, "About what?"

"HSPBs. It stands for Heaven Sent Perpetuity Bonds."

"What the 'ell are they?"

 "Well I'm not sure but…"

"What's all this got to do wi' whether or not I should trust you?"

"Because I think this Hole has some kind of incredible power to do with life and death, and possibly even rebirth, I think the Hole might be linked to some kind of afterlife."

Emily had heard enough. She sighed and turned to head out of the door.

"My own father tried to kill me for reading that stuff on his computer. He ordered my murder."

Emily stopped again. "Yer a liar, a practised liar. Rich people are always the same. They call it sophistication. In my mind that just means good at lyin' and deceivin' and screwin' other folk not so 'sophisticated', besides I never 'eard 'owt so ridiculous in me life," but her voice was uncertain. She turned and even in the darkness could see the deep sorrow etched on his face. It was too moving to be an act. She couldn't walk away.

"If what yer sayin' is true, explain 'ow the 'ell yer escaped?"

"I didn't," he replied holding her gaze, willing her to believe him, desperate for her to believe him.

At first she didn't understand. She just stood staring at him, her brain working away, digesting his words until it was ready to understand what he was saying.

"Yer tekkin' the piss," she said finally. She sounded unsure.

"I'm not. His henchmen ran me over in a car. I was murdered. The headlights were blinding and then there was a terrible blow to my body. I watched myself lying on the grass dead. I was all broken. I watched my father stand over my dead body without a care. I went to some dreadful place for the dead and somehow, and I think it's got something to do with this Hole, I returned."

"I can't gerrus 'ead 'round what yer sayin'. I can't listen ter this. Me world's fallin' apart. They're gonna' kill us brother and now yer talkin' like a madman. What's come over this place? This wur me 'ome, a safe place. Now it's corrupted by evil and I've nowhur ter go, no one ter turn ter fer 'elp," Emily could feel herself becoming hysterical. She wanted to run away from him and his story, because she was beginning to believe him.

Jeremiah could feel her hysteria. He knew she was going to run. It made him feel as tense as though he were being screwed into a tight ball and crushed.

"Argh!" It was a guttural cry and he hunched up in his chair as much as his bonds would allow.

Emily wanted to run from him but her legs were rooted to the spot.

"Argh!" He screamed again.

His agony terrified her but she could not run. Again he screamed and she watched him writhe on the chair and double over, as though he had been punched in the stomach.

"What yer playin' at?" she hissed crossly. But she was too worried to leave him. If it was an act it was good, she thought.

"It... keeps happening to me..." he gasped. "It's something to do with that..." Jeremiah couldn't finish what he was saying before another bout of pain took his breath away.

"Ter do wi' what?" she asked looking around, but she could see nothing. When she turned back to Jeremiah she found herself squinting, unsure what she was looking at. Jeremiah seemed to be shrouded in a mist. She stared again. *Was it a mist?* She wasn't sure but he was definitely becoming fainter. The more his pain increased the more he seemed to disappear from view. Emily stared at his ghostly form. Then she saw the other thing; she saw it from the corner of her eye at first.

"What the 'ell's that?" she gasped, ready to flee again as the thing came closer.

"It's... from... that... place," Jeremiah grimaced,

"where... I... was... dead. Aargh!" He cried out again and this time he became so faint she could see through him to the chair he was sitting on.

"What's 'appenin ter yer?"

But by now he couldn't speak. It was as though he was being gutted alive, except that there was no obvious sign of physical torture.

"Oh my God, it's comin' fer yer," Emily began to back away.

"Don't go," he gasped.

Suddenly he grabbed her hand. Emily screamed.

"How d'yer hands get free? Let go. Let go of me, I said." She was trying to shake her hand free as though his ghostly hand was burning her. But she was also torn. She couldn't leave him like this, in agony with that thing getting closer. The creature seemed to grow stronger and more menacing the weaker the boy became. Its skin was repulsive. She felt the bile in her stomach churn when she looked at it. She wanted to vomit. Its long shadowy arms were reaching out towards him.

Jeremiah suddenly let go of her. "Go," he hissed. "Go! Escape! Don't let it get you." He'd had a change of heart.

And so had she, "But I can't leave yer 'ere on yer own wi' it. It's cripplin' yer somehow."

Without further thought Emily picked up the knife again and made slashing movements at its shadowy feelers. She got it, got something. It began to retreat. But it wasn't so much the threat of the knife that made the sprite retreat it, began to retreat when Jeremiah's pain began to subside.

"It's goin'," Emily whispered with more confusion than triumph in her voice.

Jeremiah began to relax as the pain began to ebb, until it eventually petered out entirely and his form was solid again. When he was himself again the sprite slunk off into the background so that only its presence could be felt.

"Are yer alright?" Emily said, gently placing her hand on his shoulder. "God I've never seen 'owt on this earth like that before. Yer wur dissappearin' right before me eyes and that thing… that thing wur comin' fer yer the weaker yer got. It wur lappin' up yer pain and gettin' bolder. That creature looked like summat from Hell."

Jeremiah looked at his hands. They were still trembling but they were solid. "Now do you believe me?" he asked. He was still panting as though he'd been running for miles.

"I don't know what ter believe." She paused for thought before continuing "Aye, I think I do believe yer."

Jeremiah breathed a sigh of relief. "We've been talking too long," he said. "We need to get out of here. They'll be back looking for you now that you've escaped."

"Aye they will," she nodded and with the cuff of her jumper she wiped away tears that had spilled down her cheeks. Jeremiah grabbed her arm. She flinched again, surprised and afraid. How had he managed to free himself as though he'd done some sort of magic trick? She was still suspicious of him.

"Trust me," he said, reading her mind and holding her gaze.

"I don't knaw that I can."

"You can," he said firmly. "You really can." And he squeezed her arm reassuringly.

"I 'ope fer me brother's sake I'm not going to regret this," she said looking at his hand clenching her arm.

"You won't," he replied letting go of her.

"Right. Well it seems I 'ave no choice any road now yer've got yersell free with that invisibility trick."

"It's hardly a trick. I don't like it happening."

"Aye, well any road, I'll get yer a fleece from porch."

"Thanks," he said smiling and his smile reached his eyes.

Now she knew she could trust him.

20

Shae-nae opened her eyes when something cold and wet kept stinging the delicate skin on her eyelids. She didn't know whether she'd been asleep or unconscious but she was in darkness again and snow was covering her like a cold, silent killer. "No! No! No! Please, not here again!" she cried aloud. But nobody could hear her. "Oh mum," she sobbed. She was remembering the detail of her own death. Hot tears were spilling down her cheeks. "Oh mum," she sobbed, reliving the scene when those men burst through the door and took aim while her mother, oblivious, was slumped in the chair next to her. Had she woken when the explosive report of the gun sounded? Had her mother woken then at least and cried for her only daughter?

Shae-nae stopped crying quite suddenly. She couldn't shake the crystal clear image of her mother's drunken face from her mind. That selfish face made something cold leak from her heart and seep into her veins, chilling them, chilling her to the core, so that when it occurred to Shae-nae that those men might have killed her mother as well she didn't care. 'Good,' she thought. 'Good,' because all of a sudden she decided she hated her mother for such betrayal. Anger consumed her and she was glad that her mother might be dead. Then she became convinced of it and the idea possessed her, imbuing her with a temporary madness. Shae-nae bolted over the frozen landscape and through the trees. By the time she reached the water's edge she ached all over and her face was bleeding from scratches made by low branches.

It was as she stood at the water's edge panting, that she first became aware of its presence. All along she'd had a sense that someone or something had been running with her and now she felt it by her side. She knew somehow that it was panting like her even though it was silent. She turned, expecting something to be there, but there was nothing: nothing but the shadows of contorted winter branches, projected onto the luminous snow by moonbeams. "Jeremiah," she whispered, "is that you?" He didn't answer but she was convinced it was him. She needed to believe it was him.

Why was being dead so much like being alive, she thought? The pain of exhaustion and loneliness were not lessened at all. If anything they were worse because she couldn't do anything about them. She stared across the water, mesmerised by the moonlit ripples that slid across its cold surface like silver snakes. A biting wind blew towards her and she cursed an afterlife where you could feel the cold as though it was sharp knives stabbing you.

Was she in Hell? Perhaps she deserved it she thought, as some of her dark memories came back to her making her shudder. She needed to get moving; she needed to get warm; she needed to forget about some stuff.

Shae-nae didn't have a plan, she just ran along the water's edge hoping it would lead her somewhere. Eventually, she saw the warm orange glow of a lamp hovering above the water in the distance. The light was muted as though it was behind a screen. Some minutes later she spotted a small wooden rowing boat tied to a jetty and headed for it. She swiped the snow from the canvas cover before removing it and climbing in. Untying the rope and using the only oar that was there she pushed the boat away from the jetty. The wind was biting and her fingers burned and turned blue, but she didn't care. She figured if she was dead she couldn't run out of steam even if it felt like she was going to. So she rowed: rowed until her wrists arms and shoulders were on fire and her back ached like an old woman's. She thought of frostbite and gangrene, but what did any of that matter if she were dead?

The light got bigger but not much brighter as she neared. She was pulling up against some kind of jetty, built right out into the water. As she steadied the boat against it she heard footsteps thudding upon the boards. She looked up and saw someone approaching. *Jeremiah!* Shae-nae stopped rowing and waited before calling out. He was wearing white and looking in her direction. Instinctively, she ducked down into the boat. She would call out to him only when she was sure. The disappointment thumped her. The man she saw was dark like Jeremiah but she could tell, even from such a distance, that it was not him. He was too tall and wore plush white clothes. He smacked of wealth and power. Shae-nae shook her head and tried not to think about the strange world she was in. She just had to keep her head down and navigate her way through it. That's what she had done in life: the same applied now, in her afterlife.

Heavy tarpaulin sheltered most of the jetty and divided it into sections. She was too afraid to head for the light now. That was where the man had gone. So she rowed to the end of the jetty where there was a pontoon right out into the deepest part of the lake. She docked against it and climbed onto the wooden frame. There was no light under the tarpaulin here. It was dark, secretive and silent. Double-checking that nobody was looking, she lifted the heavy plastic and disappeared underneath. She shivered because she felt the presence and its shadow slip under with her.

The sound of silence struck Shae-nae first. The biting wind was banished by the thick tarpaulin making the silence sudden and eerie. Then it was the darkness that unnerved her. The tarpaulin was thick enough to filter out even the moonlight so that it was pitch black. Shae-nae sat on her haunches waiting for her eyes to become accustomed to the darkness. She felt safer on her haunches.

She didn't want to stand because she had a sense that she was on the edge of something, a cliff if it were possible in the midst of all this water, and if she stood she felt she would sway and fall. Eventually her eyes were just able to make out the wooden boards beneath her, at least the gaps between them. Using her hands as feelers she began to crawl across them. The boards were rough and cold. She knew she would be warmer if she stood but she didn't dare because she still had that feeling of precariousness.

She was glad that she had been so cautious when she reached one of her hands ahead of her and felt nothing. Now that her eyes were more accustomed to the darkness she could just about make out that the board immediately in front of her was missing. Blackness was there instead. Beyond that she could see more blackness; *more missing boards?* Shae-nae reached out as far as she dared but she couldn't find anything solid. It was a hole, she thought, big enough to fall down. She had been right to be cautious.

Suddenly something warm and furry brushed past her hand and scuttled along her legs: it was a rat. At that same moment she felt the presence pass over her and she couldn't help crying out. "Argh!" she screamed.

"Damn it," she cursed under her breath. It was just a rat. How loud had her cry been? She was thinking of the man in white further down the jetty. Had he heard her?

No sooner was the question formed than she heard voices, then footsteps running up the jetty towards her. Her question was answered. Shae-nae quickly backed out under the tarpaulin and clung to the cold ledge of the pontoon outside, preying that she hadn't given herself away.

On the far side of the pontoon she heard the tarpaulin swish as someone lifted its heavy curtain and climbed through. The glow of a lamp lit up a man's figure. She could tell it was not the man in white. The man's frame was magnified by the lamp he was carrying but this man was older, his shape crooked, much less impressive. The man called out in a strange accent, "Anyone thur?" There was silence. For a few moments the man swung the lamp around the empty space. Shae-nae was expecting him to leave quickly but then he too cried out suddenly and dropped the lamp. Then there was some sort of scuffle. The man jumped. "Yer little…" but before he finished his curse Shae-nae saw his crooked shadow raising some sort of baton into the air, before bringing it swiftly down and repeatedly bashing the boards with such violence that Shae-nae wondered if such actions could explain the hole in the first place. "Thur, that's shown yer, yer furry little…" she heard him snarl.

Then she realised… *the rat*, she thought, and she felt suddenly sickened.

"Goddamn it Bill, what the hell are ya' doin' out there?"

It was another man's voice. The accent was American just like Jeremiah's. She imagined it belonged to the man in white. It was odd that she'd never met an American before and now since her death she'd met two.

"Nowt Master. Just a rat, just a rat," the crooked man replied. The tarpaulin swished again and the light and the crooked figure headed back down the jetty.

Shae-nae pulled herself back up onto the boards. The men were sinister, she was right to hide from them she thought, as she cautiously crawled back under the tarp. Despite the relative warmth behind the thick curtain of plastic she couldn't stop herself shivering. That presence was still following her everywhere, making her feel even colder and more afraid. She waited for her eyes to adjust again before crawling towards a corner where she hoped there might be some spare plastic that she could wrap around herself.

For a fleeting moment, as she crawled along the freezing boards Shae-nae gave in to self-pity. Her old life was beginning to appeal to her. With something approaching affection she thought of the squalid flat her mother kept, and the damp and dirty quilt that she used to kick to the floor rather than sleep under, preferring to pile coats and jumpers over herself instead. Her lips began to tremble and her eyes began to fill with tears. She tried blinking to stop them. What was so good about her old life anyway? It was total crap, she thought trying to sober herself up, and hankering after it was just desperate. There was no point indulging an idea that her flat was anything other than the hellhole it was and if she could deal with that, which she could, then she could deal with anything.

Shae-nae slumped down onto the boards. Her hand touched something warm. It was warm liquid. It felt good on her hand and her fingers played with it. Then she felt the warm fur that the liquid had spilled from and as she put two and two together she recoiled in horror. The rat! The dead rat! And that shadow... it passed by so close, she could feel the cold air that followed in its wake wash over her. She shuddered violently but was able to contain her horror enough to stop herself from crying out loud, afraid that those men would return.

Shae-nae wiped her hand on the boards but the sticky rat's blood just smeared around her hand and now it was cold too. She whimpered under her breath, and using her foot she brushed the dead body towards the hole. She wanted to hear it plop into the water below. She did not want to share her confined space with it.

The little broken body tipped over the edge but she didn't hear it plop into the water. Shae-nae felt around the edge of the boards checking to see if she had missed the hole but its body was not there. It had definitely gone. Curious, Shae-nae sidled up to the hole and leaned over. She was listening for the sound of water slopping about below. The wind must have dropped she thought because she couldn't hear so much as a tinkle of water. The silence was weird she thought, like nothing she'd ever encountered before: deep, hollow and black as though the silence itself were breathing, as though the silence was something she could hear.

Shae-nae shuddered but continued to lean over the hole. She was sure if she waited long enough she would hear a splash of water or something, anything. She looked down into the blackness and waited. She waited for some time until she forgot what she was waiting for because the unnatural blackness began to intrigue her. A wisp of something down there caught her attention. A strange, hypnotic light suddenly began to emerge.

It began as nothing more than a pinprick of white on black at first, but then it grew and elongated and began to swirl around within the empty space. 'What was that gassy stuff?' she wondered absently. 'Was it coming closer?' Long fingers of light, like prongs, were taking shape. The fingers of light were coming closer, coming up out of the hole and reaching for her? Shae-nae blinked. Her eyes suddenly felt tired and she wasn't sure she should believe what she was seeing. But the long wisps of light kept coming closer. They really did look like fingers, she thought, and one did seem to be reaching for her. It found her hair. It was wrapping itself around her hair, lifting it, twirling it around…

Shae-nae gasped suddenly and threw herself back from the hole. She shuddered as though she had almost lost something of herself that was precious. She was about to peer over the edge to see if the gas had gone, when there was an explosive crack and bolts of light shot through her, paralysing her, as though she were being electrocuted. She was only vaguely aware of the boards shaking beneath her and the thunderous sound of a huge body of water surging, because light was burning through her closed eyelids scorching her brain and imprinting it with a terrifying image. It was an image that made her put her hands over her closed eyes and scream out loud despite the men. It was an image of her mum.

Burned on her brain was the image of a woman ravaged by the life she had chosen. A woman whose years had been accelerated by excessive alcohol, cigarettes and violence, so that she looked like an old woman and not the thirty-four years Shae-nae knew her mother to be. But her face was even worse than usual. It was bloated, so that you couldn't see her neck. Her skin was yellow and grey. Her mouth was slack from drunkenness. Deep cracks in her lips from chain smoking, and toothlessness from malnourishment made her face look puckered like that of a gummy old man. Tiny pin-prick eyes, glassy and colourless, stared at Shae-nae without seeing her. Her once glorious head of auburn hair was reduced to a few strands that were blackened with grease... and the bruises, not from boyfriends anymore, she hadn't had one of those for a long time, the bruises she sustained now were from crashing around her flat and falling over.

Shae-nae sobbed. Although seeing her mother drunk, dishevelled and bruised was nothing new to her, this image was different. It was like seeing her anew. Like seeing her through someone else's eyes, someone less numb to it. The image was shocking and heartbreaking. Her mother was obviously dead and what Shae-nae could see was her death mask. It was too potent, too horrific to bear. Shae-nae opened her eyes. She hoped by doing so she could dissolve the image, chase it away using mind over matter, but she couldn't, it was just there being projected into her brain by the light from that weird hole. Her horror turned to rage and she screamed not caring who heard. She'd always tried to believe her mother wasn't that bad. But this image, this face… this was exactly how she was. She hadn't been living anyway: she might as well be dead.

Then the image began to alter. Subtly at first so that Shae-nae didn't notice her mother's bulbous red nose beginning to grow. She didn't notice how snout like it had become until it started to twitch. Then she noticed that her cheeks were beginning to sprout whiskers and her glassy eyes were coming alive with fierce hunger. Shae-nae wailed again as she witnessed her mother's eyes turn black and her face grow fur. Now her nose was black and shiny and blood spilled out from a huge, fresh wound that deformed her hairy head. Her mother was coming for her, coming out of the hole all bloated and deathly.

"Where is my baby?" she squeaked grotesquely. Then she began to sob and sound more human. "Where is my beautiful dead baby? Shush! I can hear him crying. Oh, where is he? Where is his tiny little body?" She pleaded in a way that made Shae-nae sick with fear and sadness all at once. "Please tell me where I can find him? Oh Ganyshere, you know not what you have done. My time for revenge will come."

Suddenly the mutant image of Shae-nae's mother seemed to focus sharply on Shae-nae and an horrific grimace spread across her rodenty mouth: "Ah, Hixingel my lovely child, how wonderful to see you." Her mutant mother reached up to stroke Shae-nae's face. Shae-nae instinctively recoiled from the terrible yet familiar creature: "Come with me," her mother squeaked. "Come with mamma, I'll look after you," she squeaked again. Her jaws were agape and she was slavering.

They were words Shae-nae had longed to hear but not like this. This creature wasn't her mother. This mutant creature that talked of dead babies was terrifying. Shae-nae threw herself backwards, clamping her hands over her ears. She didn't understand what she was seeing or hearing. Was it her mother, or was it the rat that man had killed? Was it was a mixture of both, or was one being possessed by the other? She couldn't tell but whatever it was Shae-nae just wanted it to go away.

Then it did go, the grotesque face, the terrible words, the blinding light, everything... everything but the terrible memory and the desperately sad sound of someone whimpering. Shae-nae realised the whimpering was her own. She held her breath to stop herself and her body shuddered violently in protest. But at least the whimpering stopped. Silence again. The silence was profound. Shae-nae opened her eyes. The rat had gone but a light still lingered like a strobe, circling the hole like a toy train on a track, so that she could see its shape. This hole wasn't just the result of a few missing boards. It was a Hole: a big round Hole; a Hole big enough to fit a car down it; a black Hole unnaturally holding back all the tonnes of water around it, so that you could only imagine its depths. Then she looked beyond the Hole, at the thing that kept catching her eye. The thing crouched in the corner shivering. There one minute gone the next, as the strobe like light lit it, and passed it, lit it, and passed it. Shae-nae sobbed. She knew immediately that it was a sprite.

Agonising pains gripped her suddenly and she dug her fingers into her stomach. Somehow the pressure relieved the pain. But when she looked down at herself she could not see her torso, or her hands, despite the light that the Hole was still emitting. She could see the boards beneath her, and the white tarpaulin around her, she could still see the sprite cowering and looking at her out the corner of its eyes, but she could not see any part of herself. She could feel herself, her face, her stomach, and the pains deep inside, so why couldn't she see herself? What was happening to her?

Sick with fear and aching from the pains Shae-nae doubled over looking down in disbelief at the place where she knew her hands and her body should be. Then something made her look up. It was the sprite. It was no longer cowering in the corner. It was sneaking towards her like a cancer. Waiting to take her just as it had done those creatures in the queue. It was halfway around the Hole now, crouching low, sneaky and deceitful as it came for her. Shae-nae groaned. "Go away," she cried trying to kick it with her foot but only managing to cause herself more pain. The pain made her light-headed but the cowardly sprite retreated slightly as it became more wary of her.

As quickly and as inexplicably as it had come the pain in her stomach began to subside. She began to see her hands and body again, if only in short bursts at first, coming and going as though they were flickering like candlelight in a draught. Eventually, they became permanent and solid again and the pain disappeared entirely. The sprite, seemingly dispirited, slunk back to its corner.

The pain must have blinded her in some way she concluded as she looked at her hands in as much detail as possible in the dimming light. Then the light died completely and she could no longer see herself, or the sprite, or the Hole. Shae-nae slid to the floor. She decided to give up. She cried great gulping cries that took hold of her whole body and shook it as though her grief was a madman throttling her. Wretchedness consumed her. She didn't care that the strange crooked man might hear her and come with his stick.

21

*T*homas was glad he was sheltered from the biting wind and snow but he had been tied uncomfortably to a chair for what seemed like hours now. His wrists were burning and his shoulders felt stretched, as though his arms were coming out of their sockets because they were pulled too far behind his back. He was stuck inside a small dully-lit makeshift cabin with Bill. An electric lamp powered by a small generator gave the cabin light. On one side of the cabin there was a trestle table covered with a stained plastic tablecloth. It supported a kettle, a tray with some old chipped mugs on it, some dirty teaspoons, and a jar each of tea and coffee. Next to the table was a small fridge with tea stains splattered down its door. Next to the fridge was a small glass fronted mahogany cabinet, which housed crystal glasses and some vintage bottles of alcohol: a touch of luxury in the otherwise grim surroundings. Thomas was sitting on a rickety folding chair, next to a three bar gas fire which wasn't switched on.

"Me wrists are hurtin', can't yer loosen 'em a bit?" It was only the second time Thomas had spoken; the first was

179

to complain that his father was binding him too tightly, but Bill hadn't taken any notice.

"Keep yer gob shut and yer'll ger yersell into no more trouble at least."

"What no more trouble than this? That's summat any road," replied Thomas sarcastically.

Bill wheeled round and slapped his son hard on the side of the face. It came as such a shock it dazed him, and he could feel the burning pain where the welt was growing for several minutes afterwards.

"I'm in no mind fer yer sarcasm," Bill growled, but there was a trace of regret in his expression.

Bill was afraid and excited all at once. Thomas almost didn't want to know why but he had a bad feeling that he was going to find out very soon and that it was going to involve him and Emily. He thought of her crouching behind his bedroom door. She'd looked so terrified. He hoped the woman hadn't found her. Emily escaping was the only glimmer of hope he could cling to. If they hadn't found her she could find help. But halfway to the lake the woman had decided she wanted to go back to the cottage and double check. She'd said something about 'sensing the girl' there. He just hoped Emily wasn't still there and that if she was, she'd phoned the police at least.

The shock of his father's blow seemed to encourage the cold to set in with a vengeance and Thomas' teeth began to chatter. He was colder than he'd ever been, even after he'd fallen in the lake last spring, trying to rescue the Garth's dog. The icy spring water had filled his mouth and his nose and he'd thought he was drowning like the dog. Still, at least he wasn't wet like then, bitterly cold yes, but not wet.

Bill had let him grab a waterproof and some Wellington boots on the way out. Even so he wore nothing but his pyjamas underneath. The waterproof material of the coat and the boots absorbed the cold so that it felt like he was wearing cold metal against his recoiling skin. Finally, they'd arrived at the lake and Thomas was shoved under a flap of tarpaulin that represented a door to the cabin. He still hadn't seen the Hole, the cause of all the trouble. He guessed it was the bit separately sectioned off at the far end of the pontoon.

Bill noticed Thomas shivering and placed a blanket around his shoulders, before lighting all three bars on the small gas fire, something he never did at home. The warmth from it was luxurious. On the one hand, Bill seemed to want to make him as comfortable as possible, but on the other hand… Thomas thought of the burning welt on the side of his face and winced. It must be that woman, he thought. She must have corrupted him somehow. She was so beautiful. She might have Bill wrapped around her long elegant fingers, not him though, not Thomas, he couldn't stick her, he saw her evil before anything else; to him she was as ugly as a person could be. Thomas thought how he'd love to stick the gun in her face for a change. But she had gone and he was tied to a freezing cold, plastic chair, alone with Bill, a man he no longer considered to be his father.

"Would yer like a brew son?"

Thomas smirked, his father had never offered to make him a drink before in his life. "Don't call me yer son!" he hissed without thinking. .

"Aye, well, yer'll feel better when yer've got a hot drink inside yer," Bill said pretending to ignore Thomas' outburst.

"Don't bother, I don't fancy gettin' poisoned like our ma." He knew he was pushing it but couldn't stop himself.

"I 'ad ter do it. She wouldn't 'ave understood, she woulda' tried ter stop us. If yer play yer cards right wi' these people lad yer won't get yersell inter anymore trouble."

"That's what she told yer is it? Is that 'ow she managed to convince yer ter kidnap yer own son, by promisin' she's not goin' to 'urt us like? Or did she flutter 'er eyelashes and make yer some other promises me ma don't know about?" He knew he shouldn't have said it, he didn't even quite know where it came from.

Bill leapt out of his chair and hit Thomas hard across his face again but this time it was so hard that the chair flew backwards and slid out from under the tarpaulin. The back of the chair and Thomas' head were over hanging the lake. He was looking straight up at the stars and blinking away snowflakes. He could hear the water slapping the wooden stilts of the jetty beneath him. He was stuck. His hands, tied behind his back, were crushed beneath him. His heart was pounding in his throat; and his face was burning as though he'd been branded with a hot iron.

Suddenly he felt pressure on his ankles. He was being dragged back under the tarpaulin again. Bill was snarling in his face. "Yer'd better show me an' 'er some respect boy if yer want to get through this."

"Get through what? Fer all I know yer gonna' kill us any road." Thomas could taste blood in his mouth.

"They will son. You an' yer sister if yer don't play yer cards right," Bill answered as he pulled Thomas' chair upright.

Thomas was still reeling. His father had become a monster. He didn't know him anymore.

"I knew Em shouldn't a looked at the 'Ole. That's what this is about in't it?"

"Aye, Thomas it is."

"Is it oil then or what?"

Before Bill answered they heard footsteps on the boards outside. The flap of tarpaulin began to lift and Thomas watched his father stiffen. He recognised the man immediately. It was the man who'd chased him earlier. Levi Washington stepped into the makeshift cabin and fixed Thomas with his unnaturally bright green eyes, while he removed his white fur gloves. Eventually he smiled a broad smile, revealing a set of dazzlingly white teeth. They were perfect, with the exception of one diamond studded golden tooth. He seemed to like diamond encrusted gold: he wore many thick cords of it around his neck, wrists and fingers.

"Levi Washington," he said thrusting out his hand for a shake and then withdrawing it because he realised Thomas' hands were tied. He was looking for somewhere to lay down his white gloves and his smile was beginning to disintegrate. "This place is filthy!" he said unable to find anywhere clean enough. He turned on Bill, "Can't you keep it clean for chrissakes?" Then he stuffed his gloves in his deep coat pockets.

Thomas winced as his father started grovelling around, wiping surfaces and washing out cups, just to please the American. He'd never so much as rinsed out a mug at home before. Levi noticed the look of disgust that had crept onto Thomas' face and he laughed. It was a deep, powerful laugh and he reminded Thomas of a lion. He never knew a man could feel so dangerous to be around, and the dangerous man was reading him like a book.

"We have something in common you and I. I had a daddy just like him. Thought he was the man you know, always slappin' me around when I was just a kid. It made him feel big ya' know. But I showed him. I showed him *real good*. Pretty difficult to slap me around once he was in a box six feet under. You understand what I'm saying now don'tcha boy?"

Thomas was rigid with fear. Levi threw his head back and laughed. His laugh was terrifying.

Thomas stared at Bill grimly. Levi leaned in close again and said: "You wanna' see me humiliate him? You hate him enough, right?"

Thomas couldn't speak, although he shook his head vigorously. He thought he hated his father, but now he was confused. In the face of this man's threats, his instinct was to protect his treacherous father.

"I could make him lick my boots right here, right now if you like. He deserves it, you know he does."

Thomas closed his eyes. He didn't know what to say, feeling as though whatever he did or said would be wrong anyway, and then he would have to endure seeing his own father licking Levi's snakeskin cowboy boots. A shrill screech from the far end of the pontoon made Levi forget his sport however.

"What in the name of hell was that?" he cursed. "Don't just stand there you goddamn idiot," he said to Bill, "go and check out that noise." Using his cane, he pushed Bill in the direction of the pontoon. Bill grabbed a lamp and disappeared under another flap of tarp. Thomas watched the light Bill was carrying flicker all the way up the jetty towards the pontoon.

Levi turned his attention back to Thomas. "So, I expect you're wondering what it is I've got out there that's powerful enough to turn a father against his own son?" Levi pointed his cane in the direction Bill had taken.

"I'm thinking it wouldn't take much," Thomas replied pessimistically.

Levi nodded in agreement. It seemed as though he liked Thomas. The conversation fell silent momentarily as they listened to a loud thwacking noise and Bill cursing.

"What in the goddamned name of hell is he doing up there?" Levi said, but he didn't really require an answer, he was just irritated by the noise. "So Thomas, where's your sister? Emily, isn't it?"

Thomas' blood ran cold. Of course Levi didn't like him: he just wanted something from him.

The thudding noise continued. Levi lost his patience. "Goddamn it Bill, what the hell are you doin' out there?" He was becoming very agitated.

"Nowt Master. Just a rat, just a rat," Bill's voice came back.

Levi looked again at Thomas. He was smiling. "So Thomas, are you gonna' tell me where your sister is, or am I going to have to kill you?" Levi produced a shiny silver gun and aimed it in Thomas' face.

"It wur just a rat," said Bill returning through the flap. "Ere' what's goin' on? The lad ain't done 'owt."

"Shut the hell up, idiot! What do you mean it was rat? It didn't sound like a rat."

Bill was staring nervously at the gun pointed at Thomas' head. "It's not 'er if that's what yer thinkin'. Thur's nowt up thur but a flat rat and an' Hole. Nowt coulda' got past us 'ere on't jetty any road, so yer can put the gun away."

Levi seemed satisfied with Bill's explanation but he did not put the gun away. Turning back to Thomas and pointing the gun at him as though he was casually wielding nothing more sinister than a rolled up newspaper, he said: "I just want to know where the girl is that's all."

"What in God's name…" Bill cried out, as a thunderous cracking noise exploded from the far end of the pontoon, shaking the cabin as though it would break open.

Burning rods of light began shooting through the cabin. Thomas squeezed his eyes shut. The whole cabin lit up as though they were inside the heart of an atomic explosion and although Thomas felt intense heat he was not burned. The cracking noise and the sound of water surging became deafening, even so, he thought he could hear screaming, a girl screaming. He hoped it was his imagination. He prayed it was not Emily.

"It's the Hole! Clear out!" cried Levi, as he fled the cabin. Bill paused halfway through the tarpaulin flap. He turned and looked at his son and with a trace of regret he too disappeared under it.

"Hey, what about me, hey, don't leave me…"

22

*T*he jetty had finally stopped shaking and the light had gone. Thomas was too distracted to feel sorry for himself and cry; he was too busy listening to someone else crying.

"Em…is that you?"

The crying halted briefly and then continued.

"Em', it's me Thomas. I'm tied up over 'ere. Come and gerrus will yer, untie us while they're all still outside."

Silence.

Thomas saw a shadow dart behind the tarp. His heartbeat quickened, his senses flared. There was something not quite right about that shadow. Something about its ugly shape and the way it moved.

His voice felt small and it quavered, "Em?"

No answer.

The shadow loomed, hesitant at first. It reached down low. The flap lifted and the dark shadow came towards him.

Thomas believed the strange shadow had been a work of his imagination when the girl peered under the tarp. She was wild looking though and had an unhealthy grey pallor;

ghostly, he thought, except for her eyes. Even though she'd been crying her eyes were piercingly green and full of some kind of life. He felt a stab of disappointment that it was not Emily.

"Who are you?" he whispered in wonder.

"Who the 'ell are you more like it and where the 'ell am I?" she replied, sniffing the snot back into her nose.

"Did they kidnap you an' all?" Thomas asked hopefully. It would mean she was an ally and what's more she was free. She could help him.

She was really studying him. He'd never been studied so intensely by a girl before. It made him feel uncomfortable. Her eyes were filling with tears but he could tell she was fighting them back. Her chin was just beginning to tremble when she took in a deep breath, shrugged and turned away from him.

"I fought you might be Jezza." She sounded disappointed.

Suddenly Thomas felt intensely jealous of whoever Jezza was, and hurt that she was so disappointed to find him there instead.

"Gawd, I 'ate this place," she sniffed again and then continued looking around the cabin, stopping in front of the fridge: "Everyfin's weird; even the rats." She opened the fridge door. "'Ave you tried these? Are they drugged or what?" She was holding up a bottle of Evian.

Thomas was becoming increasingly unsure of her.

Asking if the drinks were drugged so matter-of-factly like that wasn't normal. Like she was used to finding things drugged. What kind of a girl was she? She must be one of them, he thought. She was still looking at him waiting for an answer.

"I, er, I don't know," he answered nervously. "Why d'yer ask?"

"'Cos I fell fa that trick before an' I dahn't wanna' fall fa it again, but I ain't 'alf got a ragin' 'first. Christ, I fought when you wos dead, you'd be... well... just dead, not walkin' about starvin' 'ungry and gaspin' 'firsty all the time.

Thomas felt himself reeling. She was as mad as a hatter, pacing around the cabin, talking about being dead. What on earth was happening to him?

"I, er, don't knaw about that," he answered weakly.

Shae-nae wrinkled her nose. *What was wrong with this kid?* "Sprite got you an' all I can see. You ain't been drugged yet though 'ave ya?"

"Me ma 'as."

"Yer ma? What, did ya both die togever or somink? What was it, a car accident?"

"No, she's back at our cottage. They drugged 'er thur before bringin' me 'ere."

"Oh," Shae-nae didn't understand. "I was shot. See the bullet 'ole in me 'ead."

"Not really." Thomas didn't really know what else to say to the crazy girl. She looked tired, exhausted, thin, hungry and pale as though she ought to be dead, but he couldn't see the faintest sign of a bullet hole in her head. He felt she might be disappointed if he actually said so.

"Oh, it's probably dried up a bit now." There was an awkward silence. "So, d'ya reckon I can drink this or what?"

"I think so," Thomas answered. "It's fer them, so they're not likely to poison it I s'ppose."

"So the sprites drink Evian now. Well that's an improvement on them potions they've been servin' up."

Sprites, what in god's name was she talking about?

"They're not sprites they're just people. Scary people mind yer."

"What's this, some kind of PC talk for sprites? Aren't ya' allowed to call 'em sprites in case you offend 'em or somink?"

"No, I really think they're just humans." Thomas answered, although he was beginning to feel unsure himself.

"Yeah, whatever. Dead humans I suppose, what's been 'ere a long time and got really well rotted."

"What d'yer mean by that? Whur's 'ere?" Thomas asked.

"Ya, know in that place. Ain't ya' been to the castle yet?"
"No."

"You ain't missed much mate. Ya' been tied up 'ere the whole time?"

"Since I were kidnapped yes."

"Mate ya' wosn't kidnapped. That's what I fought at first. You wos killed, or died, anyways. That's why ya' here in hell, or whatever this godawful place is. Ya' sprite's most probably tied ya'up before ya' came too."

God what if that were true, thought Thomas. "If by that place yer mean Darkmere, well it in't that bad," he said, feeling increasingly unsure of himself. "I'm sure it's not as excitin' as London, or whurever it is yer from but it really in't that bad."

"Is that where ya' from, Darkmere?" the name sparked a flicker of recognition but then it left her. "Where's that then?"

"The Lake District, but I'm not *from* thur, I *am* thur, right now. So are you," he replied, ignoring her look of amazement. "Look, all this is wastin' time. We need to gerrout of 'ere."

At first the girl was dumb struck; then she appeared to be lost in thought.

"Come on will yer, help us fer God's sake," Thomas cried.

Shae-nae ignored his plea. "The Lake District?" she was frowning. "Is this a lake were on now?"

"Yes! Fer God's sake hurry up won't yer."

"I'm sure I 'eard those blokes say somink about a lake."

"Who?"

"Them blokes wot chased me."

Thomas wanted to ask what men but he was conscious

192

that time was running out. "Look, tell us later. Just untie us wi' yer. We need ter ger out of 'ere."

"Maybe ya' are alive then?" she said with wonder.

"Course I am," but he was beginning to feel doubtful. What if that was why nothing was making any sense anymore? She seemed so sure. He could feel his despair growing inside him like a volcano waiting to erupt…

"Listen, fer God's sake. Just untie us will yer before they get back," he felt close to tears.

The girl cautiously took a swig of the bottled water, paused, shrugged, and then glugged the rest before taking a step towards him. Suddenly she cried out and fell to the floor clutching her stomach. Thomas watched as she rolled up into a ball of excruciating pain and began moaning like a dying animal.

"What's up, what's up wi' yer now?" he cried out exasperated. Surely the water wasn't drugged? Surely she couldn't be right?

Thomas' eyes began to fill with tears of frustration and fear. The girl was in such blinding pain it was terrifying to witness. Then out of the corner of his eye Thomas saw that shadow again, sneaking into his consciousness, no longer willing to be ignored. It wasn't a figment of his imagination at all. It was real. It was sickening to look at, with its grey skin and cracked and bloody head. Its elongated fingers grasped greedily for her, its bloody mouth was open and hungry for her. It was grotesque and predatory. It was coming for her. While she was weak it was making its move. It wanted her.

Thomas began to tremble. The shadow was getting closer to her as she writhed helplessly on the floor. It was crawling on its belly like a cat, sneaking up on its prey, moving in for the kill, while its victim was crippled with pain.

The shadow seemed less like a shadow now and more like...*like the girl*. Blood was pouring profusely from a hole in its head. Long spiny hands were reaching along the floor, its limbs stretching and gliding like water over the boards. It touched her and she screamed like a creature from another world.

Thomas could stand it no more. He screamed and closed his eyes. He was reeling. He thought he would faint. 'That creature can't be real, it can't be real, it's not real,' he told himself over and over until the thudding footsteps that were coming towards the cabin came to a halt. He opened his eyes again. Another shadow stood before the tarpaulin and the flap began to lift.

23

*E*ven with Thomas' warm, dry clothes on Jeremiah shivered. The girl didn't seem to notice the cold, she was used to it he supposed and she was walking at such a pace he could hardly keep up with her. She was brave too, like Shae-nae, or if she was not she was very good at pretending. She had every reason to be rigid with fear but she just kept going, she was going to save her mum and her brother, and Jeremiah believed she would.

As he marched, the crisp night air filled Jeremiah's lungs with a magic he had not felt for a long time. The shadow, as if sensing his vitality, retreated into the distance barely noticed. Was it getting weaker as he got stronger?

Emily too was aware of the sprite and although it seemed to have everything to do with Jeremiah, she was afraid of it none the less.

Emily stopped to wait for him to catch up: "So what's yer name then, yer still 'aven't said?"

"Jeremiah," he replied through a cloud of frosty breath.

"That's like a religious name in't it?"

"I dunno, I guess so," he answered shrugging. He'd never given it any thought before.

"Aren't yer gonna' ask us what us name is then?" she said, still waiting for him to catch up.

"Your name is Emily," he answered through a cold induced grimace. Emily glared at him. She was suspicious again.

"I saw a photograph in the house," he quickly explained. "It was you at your great grandmother's eighty-fifth birthday. Your name was written in the caption underneath."

Her suspicion cooled but they trudged on up the hill in an awkward silence. The snow fall thickened and they were unable to tell when they had reached the top of the hill, as they were virtually unable to see their hands in front of their faces. It was when they both tripped in a snow concealed depression and began rolling down hill that they realised they were on the descent.

The snowfall came to an abrupt end and sudden gusting winds temporarily cleared the clouds from the sky. The unclothed moonlight gave them a clear view at last. In between the trees that now stood between them and the lake, the water glittered like a box of diamonds. They had obviously made up a lot of ground quickly because they could see the hostages ahead weaving in and out amongst the trees. They too were heading for the lake, heading for the Hole.

Emily and Jeremiah lay in the snow for some time watching their targets until they disappeared behind a thicker cluster of trees.

"That wur me mum down thur." Emily whispered, relieved to see that her mum was still okay.

"We... should try and get... a little closer," Jeremiah added. Lying in the cold snow was making his teeth chatter.

By way of an answer, Emily climbed out of her depression and on her elbows and knees she began sniping down the hill towards them. Jeremiah followed her like a snake. They stopped in the midst of a cluster of trees. From there they could watch Iman and her hostages in relative safety, PC Birkett and Dot neared the small beach by the landing stage. Jeremiah saw the big drill towering over the lake for the first time: he'd seen enough of them to know that it definitely belonged to his father's energy conglomerate.

Emily placed a finger to her lips and pointed in the direction of Iman: "I'm gonna get closer," she whispered.

"You can't they'll see you," Jeremiah protested but she was already off, weaving between the trees until she was right on the edge of the wood and hiding behind the tree closest to them. Jeremiah came behind her silently. Now they were in earshot and for some reason their quarry had stopped.

"I can't go any further." Dot protested almost in tears.

"Get moving," Iman thundered, threatening her with the gun.

"Can't yer see the woman's exhausted, just give her a

minute will yer, then she'll be alright, just give her a little minute, fer God's sake," PC Birkett pleaded, while Dot breathed deeply.

Iman softened. What harm could another minute do? She let Dot rest.

"I'm gonna' go down thur," Emily announced.

Jeremiah laid a hand on her arm. "You can't go down there, they'll see you."

"I've gotta go, I can't wait fer that cow to shoot me own mum an' me brother."

"They'll shoot you as well if they catch you."

"Me life won't be worth livin' if me folks are dead. You go and get help. Yer'll 'ave tu go o'er Scar Fell like," she pointed at the mountain, "but once yer o'er it yer'll see the village in't distance. Go ter 2 Tarnside Lane, ask fer Sharon, say…"

Before she was able to finish, there was a thunderous cracking noise, as though a juggernaut were ploughing up out of the earth beneath them. Simultaneously, blinding bolts of light began shooting up into the sky, connecting the stars like a dot-to-dot. The light began radiating out across the night sky like spilt milk, until all the blackness of space had become blindingly white. The blinding white light in the sky became joined to the centre of the lake by an unstable and tumultuous funnel, like a tornado. It all happened in a split second.

Jeremiah quailed. He recognised the light. It was the same

light that he had fought to get to in that place, but here, now, in this place, it was angry and volatile and scared him beyond his limits. It was worse than the sprite, worse than the creatures, more terrifying than the place itself. It would destroy him if he got too close, it would destroy anyone in its path. Jeremiah looked at Iman. Her face was lifted skyward, although her eyes were closed, and she held her arms open wide in a gesture of welcome. She loved it, she was basking in it. Jeremiah thought of that picture, 'The Feeding of the Hole'. The Hole meant death and the light helped fetch it.

Two men suddenly ran out from behind the tarpaulin on the pontoon, just as the lake began to surge and rise up like a tsunami threatening to wash away those by the shore. It was Bill and Levi but Emily wasn't thinking about them as they ran with all their might to a safe distance. She was climbing her tree and watching her mother and PC Birkett, who were still standing on the shore, as though unaware of the rising water. She was about to call out to them and expose herself to danger when Dot suddenly noticed.

"The water, the water," she screamed and she began desperately trying to pull PC Birkett away. Iman noticed it too and abandoned them on the beach, rushing instead to join Bill and Levi, who by this time were climbing a ladder on the drill.

It seemed an age before PC Birkett cottoned on. Dot was yanking his arm with the handcuffs until eventually he began to run. But they were clumsy running handcuffed together and they tripped before they were far enough away. The water rose and came over them. Emily cried out as she watched her mother's gulping expression, before the surging body of water engulfed her. They were going to drown.

Suddenly there was gasping and screaming coming from further down the shore. The water had washed Dot and PC Birkett further along the shore and further up towards the trees. They weren't dead, but they weren't safe either. The water was rushing back again. PC Birkett managed to wrap his arms around a steal girder at the base of the drill and Dot hung on with him. This time when the water surged it only reached their thighs. Dot was knocked over but PC Birkett was strong enough to stop her from being dragged back. When the water came again it was only at their ankles. They had survived but they were not out of trouble. They were both soaking and in danger of freezing to death.

"She's okay, look that guy's takin' real good care of her," Jeremiah said as they climbed back down the tree. He could feel Emily's urge to run down to her mother. "If you go down there, Iman will point that gun straight at you and then you'll be no help to anyone." He was holding her back. But he was not looking at Emily's mother. He was looking at his father half way up the drill.

"They're gonna' freeze to death," Emily sobbed, but she knew Jeremiah was right. What could she do? It wasn't as though she had blankets and a spare set of clothes handy.

Emily nodded and Jeremiah let go of her. Bill and Levi had climbed down and Emily was relieved at least to see Levi put his coat around Dot. Dot's face was grim and Emily hoped her mother wouldn't shrug it off, letting her pride get in the way of her well being, as Emily knew she would have done. But her mother did not, she was too distracted and confused by all the chaos to even realise that Levi was her enemy.

Iman was laughing, "The Hole," she cried over the sound of surging water, "it has taken something, it has been feeding." She was animated, excited.

"It wur a rat," Bill said.

"Bill! What in God's name are yer doin' wi' these folk?" Dot cried in astonishment. "Tell 'em ter lerrus go wi' yer."

Bill ignored her.

"You shouldn't have thrown the damn thing in the lake you idiot!" Levi snapped. His voice was edgy and a little afraid. He'd been shaken by the explosion.

"I didn't throw it in. It must 'ave crawled in after I bashed its brains in," protested Bill.

Iman didn't care though, she was laughing. "Could you feel it, the power I mean, was it not beautiful?" Her smile was radiant.

Just as it began to dawn on Emily that Thomas was nowhere to be seen, an ear piercing scream rent the air. She looked towards the jetty. Thankfully, it was still in one piece but...another scream came: a scream so hellish Emily feared it could only be coming from someone enduring the throes of an agonising death. There was only one person it could have been: only one person still unaccounted for.

Before Jeremiah could stop her she was darting through the woods like a frightened deer. She was gone. He hoped she had not made a mistake.

24

Now that he was alone again, Jeremiah sneaked further back into the relative safety of the woods. When he looked back out from behind the tree again, the first thing he saw was the radiant smile flashing magnificently across Iman's face. It was his father that made her look that way. His father was walking towards her. They embraced and kissed. It was a long, passionate kiss, a kiss that under any other circumstances would have made Jeremiah embarrassed, but now he felt compelled to watch, to drink in every detail of his father's being: his appearance, his behaviour, everything.

The shadow sneaked closer as Jeremiah trembled from the sheer strength of his emotions: his anger; his hatred; his jealously. It had spotted a weakness in him. It could feel his growing sense of anxiety as he watched his father, and his growing sense of shame as he watched him caressing that woman. Jeremiah stumbled backwards away from the shadow, and away from his father, but a blanket of horror had already engulfed him. "Father!" he gasped and the shadow sneaked closer. A gut wrenching pain made Jeremiah cry out again because he could stand the pain no longer. He looked towards his father knowing that his cries had been heard…

Jeremiah dug his fingers into his stomach. He didn't know how much longer he could tolerate the pain. At its worst, he thought it would end in his death, although even his real death hadn't been this painful. This pain was so intolerable… he must be dying, he thought, just differently this time. Jeremiah watched helplessly as the sprite sneaked up on him, its red eyes lusty, its mouth agape and drooling with the ecstasy of anticipation. Then he heard a female voice; a voice he recognised: "Search the trees," Iman commanded. "There is someone out there." But Jeremiah was paralysed by his agony and even though he knew his father was coming for him he lay writhing on the ground unable to run away.

The sound of his father's heavy boots thudding towards him got louder as he came closer. Jeremiah was filled with the same terror as he had been on the night of his murder, when his father had chased him down the drive. Jeremiah could not think past the pain though, and he curled up on the cold ground, waiting for his father to come.

Levi was upon him in no time, searching and listening for the sound of Jeremiah's laboured breath. Jeremiah gasped as another bout of pain gripped him, then he tensed and winced, expecting his father to locate him and strike a blow. But his father didn't strike, or even aim his gun. Jeremiah looked up squinting. His father was standing over him now. He looked confused, hearing but somehow not seeing his prey. Jeremiah cried out again as his pain climaxed. This time his father lunged blindly towards him, grabbing wildly at the air. Then he was searching the trees with a baffled expression. His father couldn't see him. He must have become invisible again, just as he had been in the kitchen in front of Emily. Suddenly, Jeremiah wanted his father to know he was there. Maybe his father had been tortured by guilt all this time. Maybe he would welcome the miracle of his son's rebirth and want him back after all. Jeremiah could forgive him if that was the case. Jeremiah became convinced that it was the case.

"Father! It's me, your son, Jeremiah," he cried out through pained gasps.

Levi's face turned ashen and he began backing away, bumping into trees.

"Father…. argh!" Jeremiah tried to reach out to his father but another bout of pain forced him to clench into a ball and he began writhing on the ground again. The sprite was almost upon him now, its face evil, its long grasping fingers, reaching out to consume greedily its most precious thing. "Father don't let it take me, don't let me die again, please!"

"Who is this? Who's playing this trick?" Levi hissed.

"Father, please it's not a trick, help me please."

"My son is dead. This is a trick. My son is dead." Levi's face was drained of colour.

"No, I'm here, right here. Father please, *I'm alive!*"

"No! You can't be! I killed you! I killed you, you goddamned son of a…"

But Levi wasn't looking at the spot where Jeremiah's voice was coming from, he was looking beyond him, his face aghast, appalled. "Get away from me, get away you freak of nature. *Get away!*" He screamed.

Jeremiah felt his heart rip open and sting with such savagery, as though someone had filled up the wound with vinegar. "Don't say that father, please." But as he looked up again, Jeremiah could see that his father was still looking beyond him, at something else, his face more terrified than before. At last his father could see something, but it was not Jeremiah. It was the sprite.

The colour continued to drain from Levi's face as he watched the sprite morph into something even more unrecognisable, something even more grey and putrid. Its head was bulging grotesquely and patches of flesh were missing from its elongated jaw, so that you could see the countless rows of teeth that were set in it. Blood seeped from folds of grey slime that sealed over its eyes. It was drooling. Then growling like a tiger, it swiped at Levi's face with long fingers that were like scythes. It almost struck Levi, almost slit his throat.

Levi fell backwards in terror. His eyes rolled back showing only the whites, and he looked as though he might die of fright. Just as the sprite lunged again he managed to scramble to his feet, turn and run. Jeremiah curled into a ball and even though the pain began to subside he cried out because of a different sort of pain. He felt completely broken.

A mixture of rage and despondency consumed Jeremiah. Rage was the stronger of the two feelings. It grew inside him until it crushed the feeling of despondency and was coursing through his veins unhindered, darkening his spirit and spilling into his soul, forever staining it with an angry black ink. The sprite's face appeared out of shadow, the folds of skin over its eyes were peeled away and its cold eyes locked with Jeremiah's. Although repulsed Jeremiah could not look away and for some reason he did not want to look away. He understood its hungry glare and it did not make him afraid as it had done before. It was as though it was part of him, on his side for an instant, and in that instant Jeremiah knew that the sprite understood everything about him, even the things he did not understand himself. When the sprite was sure that his glare had been read and understood by Jeremiah, it disappeared and its face fell back into shadow. Its cold eyes had been feeding Jeremiah with something, something that changed him.

Jeremiah's thoughts turned back to his father. He felt the pains come again but he managed to suppress them this time. He wasn't going to be crippled by the pain of his father's betrayal anymore. His father was evil: he was a psychopath; there was nothing Jeremiah could do to change that. All he could do was stop wasting time hoping that his father would change. Acceptance was where Jeremiah's strength lay: accepting his father for the killer that he was. Jeremiah decided to take control. The sprite knew what he should do, channel his anger, channel it against his father, that's what he should do. He should take revenge. In the instant the thought was formed, the sprite's face came back out of shadow once more, and it snorted lustily, as though it approved of Jeremiah's plans to kill his father.

25

Emily ran full pelt through the forest. She'd never run faster: she'd never had to. She'd almost turned back when she heard Jeremiah screaming in the woods behind her. She knew what was happening to him, she'd witnessed it in the cottage, and she knew his cries of agony would draw the attention of his father. Emily tried not to think about what Levi might do if he found his dead son in the woods. Her brother was her priority, she had to go to Thomas.

She was down on the small beach near the landing stage by the time Levi and Iman were embracing. But she stalled after that, hesitating, not knowing when to make a run for the jetty. It must have been a while because when she turned Levi was re-emerging from the woods, trembling and ashen faced. Good Jeremiah had got away, she thought, and with all attention diverted to Levi, she seized her chance to run.

Emily sprinted up to the jetty and leapt over the gate for a second time. It was at this point that Bill looked up and saw her. Emily didn't know that he'd seen her: she didn't know Bill and then the woman were coming after her as she ran through the flap of tarpaulin that took her into the makeshift cabin and to Thomas.

*

Thomas was tied to a chair. He was sobbing and trembling, but he was okay: he was alive. Emily fell to her knees beside him and threw her arms around him. He was terrified but at least he wasn't hurt.

"I'm gonna ger us both out of 'ere. Everythin's gonna be okay I promise."

Thomas was shaking his head and his tears were welling up again.

"What is it Thomas, what's wrong?"

But Thomas was unable to speak, as though he was frozen with fear.

"Thomas it's okay, someone's gone fer 'elp... we're gonna' be okay," she was thinking of Jeremiah, he would be making his way over Scar Fell by now. She didn't think about the possibility that the mountain might kill him. It wasn't an option to think like that.

"Thomas what's wrong," Emily whispered when she noticed her brother's fearful fixed stare. He wasn't looking at her he was looking beyond her towards the exit. The hairs on the back of Emily's neck stood on end. She knew there must be someone behind her. She turned. It was Iman.

"Things always turn out my way," Iman said smugly,

pointing the gun at Emily. "How very generous of you to deliver yourself to me like this, how very wise."

Bill was standing beside her. Emily couldn't read his expression.

Iman grabbed Emily's backpack: "Tie her up," she said, dramatically tossing her beautiful black hair over her shoulder. "And make sure you do it properly. If I lose her again…" the barrel of the gun briefly lingered in front of Bill's nose. But he didn't need to be threatened by Iman to obey her: he was in love with her.

Bill tightened the ropes around Emily's wrists.

"Make sure you do her ankles as well," Iman snapped coldly as she searched Emily's backpack. She smiled broadly when she found Emily's knife. "Nice try," she laughed, slinging the backpack and the rest of its contents into the corner. She shoved the knife down her waistband. "This may come in useful." She was laughing to herself, marvelling how easy it was dealing with children, they knew nothing about the world, they were so naïve and that made them easy targets.

When Bill had finished, Iman checked Emily's bonds herself. "You have been a danger to this project for too long," she hissed, "and you're going to pay for biting me," she rubbed her wrist where the purple teeth marks were.

Emily had bitten Iman's wrist just before escaping. Iman had dropped the gun in the snow but Emily hadn't had time to pick it up, she only had time to run and run

211

fast. Now the gun was back in Iman's hand and she was waiving it right in Emily's face.

Iman turned towards the exit. "You," she hissed at Bill as though she hated him, "you come with me. I want you to bring the others back here. I will see to the master. He is a little shaken."

Like a sick dog, Bill followed her out of the cabin.

*

"Em? You alright?" Thomas had finally found his tongue.

Emily nodded, although she was shaken from having a gun pointed in her face. The woman seemed to despise her for reasons she did not yet understand, it made Emily very afraid of what she might do.

"Em, yer've got ter promise me yer won't scream. It's going ter happen again any minute now, and yer mustn't scream, okay?"

His trembling voice frightened her. "What? The explosion's gonna' happen again?" she asked, staring at his white knuckles as he clenched the chair. She didn't think the jetty would survive another explosion.

"No Em, not that. Summat else but I've to say it again, don't scream I don't want them racin' back any sooner than they 'ave ter?"

"But thur comin' any road Thomas. What is it, what's wrong, what's happenin'?"

212

As she asked the question, Emily saw something dart behind Thomas' back, an upright form, human possibly, but it was unclear, shadowy.

"What wur that? Summat ran be'ind yer?"

"That's what I'm tryin' ter warn yer about Em."

Now the thing was flickering behind him. Emily blinked but the flickering thing didn't go away. Emily drew her eyes away from it and looked at her brother.

"What's goin' on Thomas?" she asked but the voice that answered her did not belong to Thomas.

"Just listen to ya' bruvver will ya'..." then a groaning sound followed, as though someone was desperately trying to mask the extent of the pain they were feeling. The voice continued: "Try not ta... cry... out... okay? I'm...gonna' help if I ...can... alright."

"Whose thur?" hissed Emily, afraid of the pained voice. "Why don't yer show yerself?"

The girl moaned.

"She can't Em. She's in some kind of pain," said Thomas.

Then the shadow sneaked past Emily again.

"But she can sneak about in't shadows freakin' us out like? I don't like 'er Thomas. I don't like er one bit."

"She is real Em, at least I think she is, but that shadow, that's not 'er that's..."

Thomas' eyes were suddenly wide with fear again. He was looking over Emily's shoulder again. At first, Emily thought Iman must have returned but her brother's face was even more afraid than that. Her skin crawled. Her heart began to beat wildly. She knew there was something there behind her, she could feel it sneaking up on her, getting closer... *and the smell!* This time she didn't dare turn around.

"Thomas what is it?" she hissed, too afraid to look around, "What are yer lookin' at? Yer scarin' us."

"D..d...don't scream Em, whatever yer do just don't scream or...sh..she won't be able ter help."

Then Emily heard the girl sobbing.

"It's comin' fa me!" the girl said.

Emily felt as though she was suffocating with fear. She was too afraid to turn, too afraid to confront the thing that she could feel almost upon her. A cold fingertip touched her shoulder and Emily felt something within her die. The fingertip became several fingertips and then a whole hand gently rested on her shoulder, suddenly clamping it tightly. The agony of her fear was unbearable but something compelled her to turn her head slowly and look down at the cold thing gripping her shoulder.

It was at that moment, when she saw the deformed, noxious, grey hand clutching her shoulder, that she feared the worst for herself, Thomas and her mother. Emily knew at that moment she was no longer up against mortal men, no matter how powerful they were, they were nothing in comparison to the unknown quantity of these creatures: the one that was following the boy and now another, alongside this almost invisible girl. These creatures were not of this Earth: their reason for being unknown, their power unquantifiable.

The solidity of the world as Emily knew it melted. Everything she thought she was certain of was undermined the instant she saw that hand on her shoulder. That hand represented a new more terrifying world, a world she didn't want to know.

Slimy grey – *was it skin?* – covered elongated, gnarled fingers that were covered in loose, cheap gold rings. The fingers were curled around her shoulder and the fingertips were digging into her flesh. Emily managed to hold onto her scream, gasping faintly instead.

The creature began moving around her as though it were using her shoulder as something on which to pivot. Then it slid in front of her. She couldn't see its face, she could just see little peaks from its deformed spine sticking out through its skin, like a zip. Emily turned away. She couldn't look at its skin, she was too repulsed, and that smell, if only she could cover her nose from the stench.

Emily looked back up when she heard Thomas whimpering quietly. It was the creature that he was afraid of. It was reaching out with its extraordinarily long fingers, just like those coming out of the Hole in the etching. It seemed as though it was reaching for Thomas: that thing of the Hole was reaching for Thomas and not the girl flickering behind him like a will-o'-the-wisp.

The will-o'-the-wisp was growing and then shrinking with the same rhythm as someone's breath and her groans were almost inhuman. Then the will-o-the-wisp disappeared completely and the slimy creature reaching out for it withdrew its arms, lingering as though foiled and unsure what to do. It was the girl it wanted, not Thomas, just like that thing wanted Jeremiah.

"It's goin' ter tekk her Em and she's our only chance. She'll 'elp us if we can 'elp 'er like."

Emily understood. She'd seen Jeremiah's creature and she'd seen it off, if only temporarily, but this time her hands and feet were tied. She hissed at the creature and shrugged her shoulders to try and shake off its cold hand. The creature turned to face Emily. Emily quailed as she looked into its red eyes and saw the bloody gunge that seeped from a hole in its head. The creature hissed back at her, releasing a gassy ribbon of foul stench in her face: it was the stench of death.

The creature turned its attention back to the will-o'-the-wisp again. But the light from the girl began to change. Her form began flickering more slowly, each time appearing brighter and stronger, until it stopped flickering altogether and became sustained. Her form began to darken and take shape. The shadowy creature with outstretched arms faltered and began to shrink back, less sure of its purpose, suddenly afraid of the girl perhaps.

At last Emily could see the figure of the girl, still cramped but in a lot less pain. She was staring at the grey creature that had been sliding towards her, the terror and pain gone from her eyes. Suddenly she seemed a lot less like a victim and a lot more like someone who had a good chance of taking care of herself. The creature stopped in its tracks and appeared confused; it didn't want her like this, it wanted her weak and afraid. It began backing away, and then, as though it was a genie from a lamp that had finished granting wishes, it disappeared back into shadow.

"That's ma sprite. I fink 'it wants ta take me back wiv' it ta some place where dead people go," Shae-nae said.

Both Shae-nae and Thomas were astonished to see Emily nodding, willing to accept this incredible explanation.

"Yer believe 'er, just like that?" asked Thomas.

Emily nodded again. Jeremiah's story was gaining more credence by the second: "It came out of that Hole didn't it? Just like you did?"

Shae-nae was taken aback. She had expected more resistance from the girl but her acceptance made it easier for her to explain: "I wos murdered 'cos of somink ta do wiv' this Hole. I 'eard these two men talkin' about it. They 'ad a photo o' me, said they wan'ed to 'elp me, but then they chased me. I wos terrified, got meself cornered didn't I? That's when they shot me in the 'ead. I still dahn't understand why. It was as though they wan'ed to shut me up abaht somink but I swear ta God I didn't knah noffink. Now I'm 'ere as though I've come back ta life some'ow, 'cept that thing keeps followin' me like it's me gaoler, as if ta say 'you're still dead mate, and ya' comin' back wiv' me ta hell. It's 'ard f'ya ta believe I knah."

"Christ!" said Thomas.

Emily was nodding again. Of course she believed the girl. She was telling the same story as Jeremiah; he too had been murdered because of the Hole, and besides those creatures weren't made up, they were real.

"It's all ter do wi' this Hole. It's got some sort o' power that they want to control. I don't understand what but…" Emily shuddered remembering the etching again. "Ave a look in us bag will yer?" she said to the girl. "Thur's a picture inside I want ter show yer."

Shae-nae picked up the bag. She pulled out the black file and stared at its mesmeric black cover."

"Thur's a loose piece of photographic paper inside. It's a photocopy of an old etching. 'Ave a look."

Shae-nae saw it and pulled it out. It was folded.

"Open it up and look at it, I think it explains something about this Hole's power," said Emily, "I'll warn yer though, it's not pretty."

Shae-nae squatted next to Thomas before unfurling the picture. They both gasped in horror.

"What is this?" asked Thomas, staring at the grotesque arms reaching up and pulling down the bodies.

"It's this Hole. This Hole 'ere right at the end o' this pontoon."

"What does it mean, 'The feeding o' the Hole'?"

"I think the Hole gets some sort of power from the living. I 'eard that woman say it had been feedin' when she 'eard the explosion. Bill told 'er it wur a rat."

Shae-nae had been quiet while she was studying the picture but now she spoke up. "It wos me wot frew the rat dahn it," she was shaking her head, "I didn't do it deliberate, but I'd just put me 'and in its blood and it freaked me out, so I frew it dahn the Hole just ta get rid of it. I didn't want it anywhere near me."

"Then what happened?" asked Emily.

"It looked just like this," she held up the etching, "the light came up out of it and..." she couldn't say anymore, she couldn't explain about her mother. "But the rat was dead, I fought ya said it fed on the living."

"Maybe the rat wasn't quite dead..."

"It wos well and truly dead I'm telling ya."

"...or maybe it feeds on the soul, who knows, but it has some power we've yet ter understand and that power seems ter require bodies alive or dead fer some reason."

Thomas sobbed quietly. Emily hated being so blunt but there was no time for pussy footing around with the facts.

"Shush!" Shae-nae suddenly fell silent and put a finger to her lips. "I can 'ear voices comin' closer," she whispered.

"Untie us then, quick," gasped Thomas, "before they get 'ere."

"There ain't enough time," she replied, "They dahn't

know I exist yet, they're not lookin' fa' me. If I get caught you've got na chance. I'm gonna' hide and wait for a better opportuni'y."

"No don't go," pleaded Thomas, "yer've got plenty o' time."

But the footsteps were already on the jetty.

"I've gotta ga mate."

"It'll be too late if yer go," cried Thomas, "Thur'll throw us down that Hole and it'll be too late!"

Shae-nae looked sorry as she slipped back out under the tarp.

Thomas wept: "I just wanna' go 'ome."

Emily didn't know if the girl would ever come back, all she could do was hope that Jeremiah had made it back to the village and had raised the alarm.

26

*L*ike a sleek animal Jeremiah moved through the trees, before sniping across the ice and snow towards the water's edge. He'd forgotten to go for help. His need for revenge consumed him so that he hadn't even thought of it. Jeremiah climbed underneath the jetty, clambering over the supporting beams until he was at the end, facing the pontoon. He was looking down into the deepest, coldest part of the lake. The water was slapping the side of the thick wooden supports, still using up the energy created in the explosion. Jeremiah closed his eyes and imagined his father's face when his dead son stood before him, intent on revenge. He would strike fear into his heart. It was an important part of the plan to see his father afraid of him.

Jeremiah climbed up onto the pontoon and underneath the tarpaulin covering it. The darkness was eerie, the silence peculiar, as though it were a noise after all, like a breeze, except that he felt none. It felt like he was in a void, a place where senses were baffled completely. Jeremiah was too afraid to move, or even stand, as though he was on the edge of a precipice. He sat on his haunches shivering, waiting for his senses to become accustomed to the darkness.

"Jesus! I can't see a goddamn thing!" he cursed under his breath. His teeth were chattering again.

"Whose there?" a scared voice came from the darkness.

Jeremiah's heart skipped a beat. He stayed silent. He could hear someone breathing quick, shallow breaths. Someone was there, someone who was afraid.

"Whose there?" the voice whispered again.

It was the voice of a girl.

"Emily is that you?"

"Jezza?"

"Shae-nae?" Jeremiah's heart began thudding with excitement. "Shae-nae is that you?"

"'Course it's me. Oh Jezza, fank god, I've bin so afraid."

"Me too. Jeez Shae-nae, I thought you hadn't made it, I couldn't find you. Stay there, I'm coming over to you." Jeremiah began to crawl forwards. "Say something so I know where you are."

"No wait!" In her excitement she had forgotten to warn him about the Hole.

"Argh!"

"Oh no, Jezza!" she gasped. Then she heard his body thud back onto the boards. "Are ya' alright? I forgot ta tell ya' about the Hole."

"No... I'm... I can't... argh!"

"Stay there, I'm comin' over." Shae-nae navigated her way around the Hole on all fours. "Where are ya'?" She said, trying unsuccessfully to reach him. He'd gone. Maybe he'd fallen down the Hole after all: "Jezza, Jezza!"

"Argh!"

"Oh Jezza, fank god ya' still 'ere." She brushed his arm briefly but then he was gone again. "Where've ya' gone again…what's up?"

"Ah… the… pain… It's happening again. It's happening more and more… ah… often."

Shae-nae sat on the floor next to him waiting for his pain to subside. "Not you an' all," she said resignedly. She knew it wouldn't last, at least she hoped it wouldn't. Her episodes didn't, even though they were getting longer, and each time she felt less able to breathe, as though she was never going to recover.

When Jeremiah stopped groaning, she reached out to him in the dark and felt his form, it was solid again. In a moment of relief she shuffled her body closer and hugged him tightly. The experiences they shared had changed her. Hugging someone, as she was doing now, was something she could never have done before, not even when she first found herself in that place. She hadn't even liked Jeremiah when she first met him. But so much had passed between them since then: so much had hurt and confused them, tortured them and terrified them. They were bound by something that was too deep for others to comprehend: only they understood.

"It's bin 'appenin' ta me too, the pain that is. Are ya', okay now?" Although he didn't answer, she could feel him nodding. "Jezza, I ... I don't know 'ow ta tell ya' this but, well, I fink I'm only 'ere fa a little while longa'. I got a sprite. It's gettin' more darin'. I fink it wants ta take me back, especially when I 'as those pains like what you just 'ad. I fink it wants ta take me back ta that place." She could feel Jeremiah nodding.

"I've got a sprite too," he managed when he was strong enough again. "You just can't see it in here because it's too dark."

"You an' all? God Jezza, what does it mean? We're knackered ain't we? We dahn't 'ave much time left but I dahn't wanna' go back there. It wos 'orrible, I can't bear the darkness, it's too much it's... I can't..."

He too began to tremble at the thought of that dark place, with its violence and the abstract ways that he could neither understand nor comprehend. Shae-nae was sobbing. He felt like doing the same but he knew it was more important to comfort her. This time Jeremiah put an arm around her and squeezed her tightly. He didn't want her to lose it, he needed her to be strong, but at the same time he knew that it was too much for them both to bear. If she was right and he only had a short amount of time left he had to do some stuff, some stuff that would help him get through his afterlife. He would help Emily and her brother and then he would take revenge on his father.

The certainty of going back made Jeremiah buckle. She was right. Shae-nae was right, their return to life was only temporary. That's why he'd never really felt alive, because in truth, while that thing was there, shadowing them, waiting, growing stronger while they grew weaker, they never really were alive. A burning desire drove him though, as it had never done before, it was enough to sustain him for now. After that, once his father was dead, and the desire to take revenge was gone, then the sprite might as well take him: there would be nothing left anyway.

"That light, the one that brought us back to life, it showed me stuff about my death. It showed me that my father had me murdered. He put me in that place Shae-nae, and if I've gotta' go back he's coming with me, or so help me..."

"It showed me somink an' all," Shae-nae added. "It showed me that two posh blokes killed me wiv' guns while me muvvar did noffink."

Suddenly she felt Jeremiah sit bolt upright and loosen his arm around her shoulder.

"Wait, let me get this straight, you didn't die accidentally, you were murdered too?"

"Yeah."

"Why? Can you remember?"

"They wos askin' Freddy, our local dealer, if 'e knew me which 'e did, 'cos me muvvar was always callin 'im up fer a bit o' this an' that, I didn't know them though. They looked powerful ya' know. I couldn't understand what blokes like that wos doin' lookin' fa' me. I knew it weren't the police 'cos I 'adn't been in trouble wiv' 'em for a while. Anyway, Freddy was givin' it the 'who wants to knah' routine, when they shoved a bloody great handgun up his nose. He tried ta leg it but they put an 'ole in his back. Shot 'im dead, just like that, right under me nose. I got scared, I was hidin' behind a wheelie bin, I panicked and knocked it over tryin' ta do a runner. That's when they spotted me. It wosn't long after that they...well ya' knah...Bang! Anyway, that's pretty much the size of it."

"Jesus!" Jeremiah shook his head sadly.

"D'ya knah? Me muvver just sat there the whole time. Lousy drunk!"

"God, I'm sorry." Jeremiah was moved.

"When I first 'eard 'em talkin', before I realised I wos back outside Tower Heights, I remember being scared by wot they wos sayin' an' I wos finkin' we musta' bin on the brink of a world war or somink. I just can't remember the actual words."

"Try!"

"I can't. I've fought abaht it over an' over, an' I just can't remember the details, it wos like a dream."

"If it's not about what you know, it must be about who you are."

"*Me?* Who the 'ell am I that makes two posh blokes wanna' murder me? I ain't done noffink, noffink that bad anyways, not for ages," secretly she was panicking, recalling a few best forgotten memories, processing them quickly to see if they were bad enough to warrant her murder. She didn't think so, but you never really knew, not there in Tower Heights where small stakes seemed high and life was cheap.

"I don't think it would matter if you were a saint or sinner, they'd still be looking for you. There must be something about *you* that's important to them, something that could threaten them."

"Nah! There just ain't no reason at all. I've been rackin' me brains and I can't fink of a thing. It don't make na sense."

"You're right, it doesn't add up but neither does finding ourselves here in the Lake District. I mean what are we doing here of all places? It's because of this Hole. We were murdered because of this Hole. It's because of this Hole that we have to go back. What if we did something about it so that we didn't have to go back?"

"Like what?"

"What if we found a way to close it?"

A flicker of light escaped from the Hole and slid around its circumference. They watched the golden beam circle the Hole gracefully, illustrating its size and pitch-blackness. They watched it suspiciously, feeling as though it was a sign that the Hole had heard them and understood their threat, as though the light was a warning to them.

"It knahs. It understood ya," whispered Shae-nae.

Jeremiah was holding her arm tightly, watching the

light suspiciously: "Shae-nae, there's something I haven't told you yet."

"Wot is it Jezza?"

"It's about my father. He's a part of this."

"What d'ya mean?"

"He's at the helm of this operation. He has to be at the helm of everything, I wouldn't be surprised if he ends up at the helm of the world."

"Ya farver's part of this? Christ!"

"He thinks he's Lord God Almighty. He's somewhere here now and he's going to kill a girl called Emily and her brother."

"I know em, I met 'em just before. He can't kill em, they're just kids."

"So were we."

It was true, but how unlike a kid she felt after everything that had happened.

"We have to help them," Jeremiah pulled her arm. "Come on let's get closer to the cabin and listen."

They climbed out from under the tarp and lowered themselves down onto the beams below.

27

*T*hey came into the cabin one by one; Dot, still wearing Levi's coat, then PC Birkett, Bill and Iman. Finally, Levi stepped in. He no longer looked ashen and seemed recovered since his experience in the woods. As he towered over them, dusting the snow off his white cashmere sweater, he looked more powerful than ever. Without taking his luminous green eyes off Emily, he ordered Bill to pour him a drink. He downed the bourbon in one gulp, gave a satisfied sigh and held the glass aloft for a top up. Bill poured in another couple of fingers without hesitation. Again Levi downed it, grimacing from the burn it made in his throat, but all the time he fixed Emily with a stare that left her feeling very cold.

"At last," he said smacking his lips and placing the empty tumbler on the floor. "We have you." Emily flinched as he fingered a straggly wave of her long tousled hair. "It's hard to believe I'm supposed to fear you; hard to believe that you, with your small girl's frame, could ruin everything."

"What am I supposed ter 'ave done?" she asked, wondering how a man who virtually controlled the President of the United States could fear her.

Levi did not answer.

"You are the true master now," Iman said stroking Levi's shoulder.

Levi was nodding: "But we can't take any chances."

"Nothing stands in our way. The others are dealt with. No one can help her now."

"What d'yer mean, the others are dealt with?" asked PC Birkett suspiciously.

"I think we owe them an explanation at least," Levi answered, his gold tooth flashing in the light of a lamp.

"Maybe I can explain," Iman said.

"Explain why yer've kidnapped a decent law abiding family, and an officer of the law? I doubt it," snorted PC Birkett.

"Let me try anyway," Iman persisted coolly.

"If yer must make excuses," snapped PC Birkett, staring angrily at her.

Iman ignored him and continued: "There is a group of people that exist today, known as Kinsmen, who believe that…" she paused trying to think how best to summarise what she wanted to say, "they believe that there exists here on earth, a direct means of access to the afterlife."

"What she means is that we, the Kinsmen, believe that the gates of Heaven exist here on earth," Levi added.

"Heaven, afterlife, it amounts to the same thing. The point is we have found that 'gate'. I think by now you all know what I'm talking about."

"I haven't got a clue what yer..." Dot was about to go into a lengthy tirade about hocus-pocus and gobbledegook when she noticed that Emily, Thomas and PC Birkett were not only silent, but very pale.

"Yer not goin' ter listen ter this clap trap are yer?" she gasped.

But neither Emily nor Thomas replied. They were thinking of the sprites, and the children they had come for; they were thinking of the missing tourists and the dead dog; and they were thinking how Iman's explanation created a link between all these strange occurrences. Even PC Birkett, was thinking of the boy in the gorse, near Fell Side cottage and how he kept disappearing right before his very eyes. He'd managed to convince himself it was a work of his imagination but now...

"Five years ago Levi," Iman nodded at him and smiled, "gave me the task of finding a tear in the black curtain of space. I did not realise straightaway that a beautiful light that I had found in space many years earlier was the very thing they were looking for. The light, my light seeped out from the tear in space, signifying its whereabouts. I hadn't noticed the tear before, it was invisible from a certain angle. But from another angle the tear looked like a perfect black disc in space, of course it was the Hole.

The Hole was heading towards earth at a phenomenal speed. I tracked the Hole as it travelled closer to our earth through space and time, and as it came closer I saw something deep inside it. I did not believe what I was seeing at first but I knew if my eyes were to be believed that I had made the most incredible discovery. Deep inside the Hole was a new planet. *A new planet!* Do you even realise how phenomenal such a discovery is? But that wasn't all. There was more. I began to study the planet and that was when it hit me. The new planet was familiar. The new planet was earth itself."

Iman waited for her audience to figure out what she was saying. They remained silent. She couldn't decide whether they didn't understand the implications of what she was saying or whether they were just too dumbfounded by her revelations. So she continued, not waiting for their minds to clear and their questions to form.

"I could see the dark continents of Africa, Australasia, Europe, America, Asia, all there and all exactly the same shape. But this planet earth was not the colourful, living, breathing earth that we know: it was a much darker version and it was cold and covered in snow. It was the earth in negative, earth in another universe, another dimension of earth entirely.

Day and night for five years I pondered how this could be possible. I concluded that, somehow, part of earth got sheered off during its creation, but not a visible part like a huge chunk of its mass; this missing part left no obvious mark upon the earth because the missing part was another dimension. Instead of one earth existing with many dimensions and layers, somehow the dimensions got separated and began to evolve separately."

Emily felt the cold finger of dread tracing a chilling path down her spine.

"It is too big to comprehend is it not?" Iman added.

"It sounds like utter rubbish and I still don't see what any of it has ter do wi' the afterlife," said PC Birkett.

Iman continued, "The Kinsmen had been trawling my homeland in the Iraqi desert for years looking for a cave believed to be near the original site of the Hole."

"What d'yer mean the original site o' the Hole?" snapped PC Birkett sceptically.

"The Hole has not always been in space. It once before existed here on earth. Eventually we found a cave that proved it." She smiled at Levi as though she was reliving the triumphant moment. "The cave's walls were covered in elaborately painted glyphs and beautifully painted text. The pictures and tales told the whole amazing story of the Hole and its effect on the ancient race that came into contact with it. We photographed the glyphs and writings and e-mailed them to Bill who translated them all with astonishing fluency. Curiously, he said they were easy to translate because he had written them. Afterwards, when quizzed about this claim, he denied ever saying it. It was something we came to understand only later." Iman smiled: Bill didn't, and there was an almost missable trace of regret, depressing his naturally heavy brow.

"Now I knaw yer all stark starin' mad," Dot interrupted. "We don't even 'ave a computer and he wouldn't even know 'ow ter switch one on if we had, let alone 'ave the ability ter translate ancient text."

"I 'ad it installed in us barn, I didn't want the kids interferin' wi' it," Bill explained, to Dot's astonishment.

"With Bill's help we learned everything we know about a race of people known as Galadrilites. As far as we know, these are the first ever people to have encountered the Hole when it first came to our earth. They were an ancient race of civilised people who were ruled by a body of people known as the Xiu Hieroniti, or 'True Masters'.

"Look, we don't need an' 'istory lesson, we can go ter university for that, just tell us what all this 'as got ter do wi' us. I don't want ter 'ere bout some ancient folk that mean no more ter me than dust."

"Some tourists went missing on this lake recently didn't they? Is it not your job to find out why?" she left the question hanging in the air for a moment.

PC Birkett hated to admit it but she was right, it was his duty as a police officer to listen to what she had to say.

"The scriptures tell us that the Galadrilites believed the Hole was a devil, or rather, it was the mouth of a devil waiting to be fed. They were terrified of it, afraid of the blackness inside it and the deep unknown destination that it led to. A master named Eviathan believed they had to feed the Hole to make it go away and because it was a devil only human flesh would suffice. They practised Human sacrifice on a grand scale."

Emily was beginning to understand the etching she had seen but understanding it made her even more afraid.

"…But the Hole did not close its mouth and go away, and the sacrifices became more desperate as the population dwindled. One of the glyphs we found in the cave illustrated a new born baby being ripped from its mother's arms and thrown down the Hole." Iman paused momentarily as she remembered the illustration. Even she had been shocked at the time. "But still the Hole showed no signs of closing… then something else started to happen."

"Some o't dead started ter return," Bill interrupted.

Iman was nodding but she let Bill continue.

"They told tales of an afterlife, but it wurn't a beautiful afterlife, thur stories wur often terrifyin', 'bout the cold and darkness, murder, torture, loneliness. And they wurn't alone in that turrifyin' place: they described other creatures; grotesque beings who, despite thur deformities, reminded 'em of 'emselves. Some o' them grotesque creatures managed to find thur way back ter this earth an' all."

Thomas and Emily exchanged a knowing look and Levi was frowning as he stared into the bottom of his empty whisky glass.

"That's when the dead and the living started to get a bit mixed up," Iman continued. "Even though 'unions' between the living and the dead were strictly forbidden by the Xiu Hieroniti, and punishable by execution, they still happened. Any children, or 'demons' as they were called, born from such unions were also executed. But such is the way of life that the moment a thing is forbidden, its value increases and the desire for it intensifies.

Katchua was one such woman. Sacrificed to the Hole at nineteen, she returned, perfectly preserved and highly desirable. It came as no surprise that demon children were born to her despite the laws. She was lucky though. She was, along with her children, afforded protection from execution. Her prior death and her children's demon heritage was a closely guarded secret because Katchua's two lovers were powerful Xiu Hieroniti: Tanimesh the scribe, with whom she had two daughters; and Eviathan, the Master who had originally ordered the human sacrifices: with him she had two sons, one of whom died at birth.

Katchua's way of life did eventually become threatened, however. She had a rival for Eviathan's affections. Ganyshere was also a powerful Xiu Hieroniti and a high priestess. She did not approve of Katchua's relationship with Eviathan and she did not approve of their demon offspring. She did not like the risk the children's identities posed to her lover Eviathan. Ganyshere ordered Katchua out of town or she would have the children murdered. Katchua had no choice. She agreed to leave for the sake of her children. Isolated in the desert however, with little to distract her from her grief over the death of her newborn baby son, she began to go insane. She returned to the city to search for her dead baby, whom she thought she could hear crying behind the city walls. Whilst searching for the source of the crying she began talking loosely to strangers about the heritage of all her children. The rumours that her children were demons born of powerful Xiu Hieroniti spread like wild fire and Eviathan and Tanimesh feared that the scandal might lead to their execution if they allowed her to continue with such talk. So they ordered Katchua and her children to be sacrificed to the Hole. The morning after Katchua and her demon offspring were sacrificed the Hole had gone."

"I still don't understand what any o' this has ter do wi' me?" Emily protested fearfully.

Iman fell silent momentarily. She was thinking. At length she faced Emily with an answer, "Have you ever been mistaken for somebody else?" Iman asked her. "Or, have you ever mistaken a stranger for someone you know? Have you ever tapped a friend on the shoulder and been surprised when someone entirely different turns to face you, someone different yet with exactly the same hair, same build, or maybe the same clothes?

"I once searched an embassy party high and low for my sister, whose laughter I kept hearing penetrating the sound of music and chatter, but when I eventually found the source of the identical laughter, the woman to whom it belonged could not have been more different. She was old and frail and ugly and my sister was none of those things; yet I could not stop staring at this woman, and I could not accept that her laughter was not my sister's. I noticed she flicked her hair in the same way as my sister every time she laughed; she even had the same twinkle in her eye. You must have experienced similar coincidences that have left you baffled."

Emily was thinking of the time a toothless old woman had grabbed her shoulder in a supermarket once. The old lady had called her Anna and tears had welled in her eyes as she stared at Emily. Emily just assumed the woman's eyesight was poor and that she was a tiny bit crazy. Then there was that other time when she and Thomas were searching the crowds for Bill at a traction engine rally. They both saw the man with his back to them, both thought he was Bill. Thomas had reached him first and tugged at his coat from behind. Emily had been ridged with surprise when a complete stranger turned angrily and sent Thomas packing.

"What if I told you though, that they were not coincidences?" Iman continued. "What if I told you these people *are* known to you in some way and that is why you are instinctively drawn to them. I told you there was at least one other dimension of earth, what if I were to suggest to you, that there were other dimensions of people: other dimensions of you, your brothers, your sisters, your mother, father, friends. Most of us have in existence right now other dimensions of ourselves. Further, most of us had other dimensions of ourselves existing in the past, and even in other dimensions of earth.

Our different dimensions are united by one thing: our soul. Our *soul* exists in other forms and in other times, even though we may not be conscious of it. The physical birth that signals the start of our life, does not always signal the beginnings of our soul. New souls are being sparked into life all the time of course, but souls can also be many thousands of years old. Once a soul is sparked into life it rapidly evolves and expands, living in a myriad of forms in this universe and others, in this time and in times gone by."

Suddenly Iman's solemnity was replaced by laughter. "This Hole and the scriptures on the cave's walls, have revealed to us a rich tapestry of life and death that we could not even have dreamed of before. I am lucky enough to know another who shares my soul and I know one who shares yours," Iman nodded at Emily.

"Three and a half thousand years ago, a girl named Odalak lived. She was a daughter of Katchua and Tanimesh the scribe, a daughter of the living and the dead. She had the power to control the Hole, when no other could."

Emily was shaking, her instincts told her none of this could be true, but she couldn't stop thinking of that picture Jeremiah had told her about; an ancient picture, apparently of her in a cave in Iraq, "I don't believe you," she managed to say anyway.

"What if I were to tell you that you and Odalak share the same soul? Odalak was able to travel between two dimensions of this earth, even after the Hole was closed. We think this may have helped her."

Iman pulled from her blouse the pendant of white gold light that Levi had given to her five years earlier. Emily squeezed her eyes tightly shut but the blinding white light penetrated her eyelids anyway. It was so bright, the light bleached the contents of the room. It took a while for her sight to adjust and see that Iman was holding up a clear container. Trapped inside it was the most beautiful light. Emily's heart fluttered with excitement. It was as though she'd seen the light before and yet, no matter how she teased her brain, she could recall no specific memory of it.

"Rather than not belonging to either the living world or the dead world, it appeared Odalak and her demon siblings actually belonged to both worlds, and were able somehow, to harness the power of this light and use it to travel between the two dimensions, even when the Hole was not there. This light is the connection between the two dimensions. It is some sort of superhighway between life and the afterlife."

Iman tucked the pendant back inside her blouse. "The light takes us to that Dark Earth where our soul exists on another level, even after this mortal earth has given us up. Imagine the enormity of this discovery. Imagine what we could do if we harnessed the power of this light… *this Hole*."

"It sounds like Hell," snapped Emily. "And I don't believe any of it," she added even though, in truth she believed it all.

"Let me finish and you will see beyond doubt," Iman smiled at Emily. "Katchua's children used the light to return to our earth after the Hole had closed. They went back to live in the cave. They found Tanimesh living there. Motivated by his terrible feelings of guilt, Tanimesh had covered the walls of the cave with intricate illustrations and writings, all relating to the Hole and the murder of his children and Katchua. They were his confessions.

Tanimesh and the children put their differences aside and decided to live in exile in the cave, forever. Unfortunately, they were discovered and so were the dangerous confessions, revealing the truth about Eviathan, Tanimesh and their 'demon' children. Tanimesh and the children were arrested along with Eviathan and Ganyshere. They were not executed however. So that they could no longer speak of the Hole, or the dead, or the creatures, or anything surrounding those terrible dark years of feeding and sacrifice, they had their tongues butchered out of their mouths.

But you know that already don't you Emily?"

Emily winced as she dug her teeth into the thick scar on her tongue."

"Show them yours Levi."

Levi stuck out his tongue as far as it would go. An ugly thick and gnarled, white scar ran all the way around the base of his tongue. Emily recoiled in horror and a cold dread seized her. She began to tremble.

"I'm Eviathan," he answered sinisterly.

"I am Ganyshere," said Iman, thrusting out her tongue to show that her scar was the same.

"Bill?" prompted Iman,

Emily turned away. She didn't need to see Bill's tongue; she knew what would be on it and she knew it meant he would be the one called Tanimesh. Emily dug her teeth into her own scar again and remembered her father's delight when it had first appeared. She hadn't understood it then, when she was just three and it was just a feint, delicate thread of a thing. She barely understood it now. Did it mean she was one of them?

Thomas darted a frightened look at her, he'd made the connection. They'd often studied her mysterious scar together in the mirror, imagining her previous lives, imagining she'd had her tongue cut out by pirates or some such thing, she could never have imagined how close to the truth they were. Thomas didn't have one. He was not one of them.

"Finally we understood the scars on our tongues, and why Bill said he wrote those scriptures, even though he did not understand it himself. It was because he did write them, at least another dimension of him wrote them."

"I can't stand this anymore," whimpered Dot.

"So what if I am another dimension of that girl, it doesn't mean 'owt."

"It does though," answered Levi. "The scriptures prophesied that you would be born and that you would wield a phenomenal power over the Hole and I'm afraid that makes you my worst enemy. Bill, tell her what else the scriptures said."

"The Hole wants ter tekk yer back wi' it. It wants ter tekk back the blood that belongs ter it. It wants ter tekk yer back ter Dark Earth wi' it." His face was scornful as he pointed at Emily. "It's come 'ere fer yer. It wur comin' fer yer before yer wur even born. I'm not gonna' stand in its way."

"Don't yer dare talk ter our lass like that yer ravin' lunatic," screamed Dot.

Thomas was shouting something too and so was PC Birkett.

Emily could hear nothing: nothing but her own words as she cried out amidst the fervent protests: *But... but... that's ridiculous. It can't be... I don't know 'owt. I don't know 'ow ter control the Hole. If I knew that... if I knew... then I'd close it now and stop all this nonsense.*

Only Levi heard her words over the melee: "You see that's the kinda talk I'm afraid of," he whispered in her ear leaving her feeling very cold. "That Hole won't serve me until I give it what it wants. Once you are destroyed, then it will be my slave and the power of this Hole will be mine."

*

Sitting on the beams underneath the cabin, Shae-nae and Jeremiah were comparing the scars on their tongues in the moonlight. Their scars were virtually identical. They heard everything. They understood things now that had made no sense to them before.

"Ya wos right Jezza, it is about who we are."

"That's why we were murdered," Jeremiah felt the words sticking in his throat.

"Some'ow we're rela'ed ta that dead woman's kids. That's why they got rid of us."

"We're not just related, we *are* that dead woman's kids and we're back again, just like last time."

"We're back an' they dahn't realise it."

"They haven't thought it through."

*

"Then what?" snapped PC Birkett. "Then what happens when yer've sacrificed 'er, we all just go 'ome and ferget about it?"

"I'm afraid none of you will be going home ever again," Levi stood up and grabbed the bottle of bourbon, before sitting back down with it and pouring another large slug of it into his tumbler.

Iman came towards him and tentatively placed a hand on his shoulder. "Come and see it now. Come and see the Hole my love. It's beautiful." She tried to take his hand but he shoved her off.

"This Hole will undoubtedly make me the wealthiest

and most powerful man in the world. I will control the gates to Heaven for chrissakes." He said it as though he could hardly believe it himself. "Obviously we need to jazz it up a bit: add a misty stairwell; some pearly gates; maybe play some sort of heavenly music. You know, make it more convincing. It'll be stylish though, with a real contemporary feel. Then, any one with around two hundred and fifty thousand dollars to spare can buy one of my Heaven Sent Perpetuity Bonds and be guaranteed the perfect afterlife.

With the purchase of an HSPB, the fear of death that we suffer with all our lives will dissolve," he laughed. "Imagine being able to buy a bond that guarantees you will be reunited with your loved ones after death. Imagine the pleasure that could be had in life if you could be sure that in the end, after death, things would only get better.

The face of the world will change. Think about it. The population's newly purchased feelings of immortality will drive an irrevocable change in the dynamics of the whole world. Our survival instincts will extend to preserving our afterlives as well as our lives. The desire to buy an HSPB will be everyone's primary motivation in life: no bad thing in my view, I can't abide sloth. Religion will be put out of business, at least there will be a new kind of religion, a universal one, one where everyone recognises and worships the power of this Hole.

But what do I care about that. I only care that I control the Hole and all who enter. I will be untouchable. Even your

Queen will be coming to me cap in hand," he rubbed his hands together and chuckled childishly.

Emily thought she was going to be sick and she felt very light headed suddenly.

"So this is all about money then, thurs no higher purpose?" PC Birkett managed to ask, but even he was trembling by now.

"You could say that a spiritual search has turned into a commercial one. It's very expensive to go around digging up other people's countries and taking for yourself things that truly belong to them. It takes a lot of money and a lot of power; you need to convince people that they're grateful for what you are doing."

"But two 'undred and fifty thousand dollars is too much!" shrieked Thomas. "What about folk who can't afford it? What pleasure will they get outta' life knowin' they can't afford ter buy an afterlife?"

"As I said, I can't abide sloth," replied Levi callously.

"Just because somebody isn't rich, doesn't mean they're lazy," protested Thomas.

"Hey so what! I'm not running a charity here," snapped Levi, taking another big slug of bourbon.

"It's not about the money," Iman hissed. "We appreciate its power…" she added dreamily.

"We appreciate its power to print money," Levi scoffed. "The fear of death exists in all of us. With a massive publicity campaign I will exploit that fear beyond measure so that it seriously interferes with the quality of people's lives. Death will be viewed as a terminal illness. Those who can will purchase the 'cure', so to speak: those who can't, well…" Levi just shrugged.

"My campaign will leave no one in the world untouched. This Hole is the biggest most powerful commodity the world will ever see. It is a guaranteed gateway to Heaven. Everyone in the entire world will share the same one and only desire: the desire to procure enough money to buy one of my bonds and secure their afterlife. Medicine is not yet advanced enough to prevent our deaths, so this is the next best thing isn't it? Within a few months, everyone will become accustomed to the idea of buying a solution for death."

"What if they don't? What if they don't believe the hype!" snapped Emily.

Levi threw his head back and laughed. "Not believe the hype, are you kidding? Mass apathy and the vast oppressive power of media will make it impossible for me to fail." Levi staggered slightly as he took another slug of bourbon.

"The simple fact is people won't want to question it. They would rather just accept things the way they are because it's easy, because being bothered would require effort. How d'ya think the Holocaust happened? The tide never turns. People don't change. Big business thrives on that kind of mass apathy and so will I. The world is only one fragile step away from another Holocaust and you have only yourselves to blame." Staggering slightly, he took another big swig of bourbon.

"And what's more, I'll be making a promise with substance. How hard do you think it will be for me to make people believe a ticket to Heaven is an essential "must have" item? Besides, not believing will just be too inconvenient, too challenging, too scary. It would involve accepting the finality of death, and nobody wants to accept that, so nobody will. That is why people will buy my HSPBs in their billions."

Emily was reeling. She felt as though she were in the thick of Hell with no sign of escape. In the end she was just a girl in the face of this unquantifiable commodity. She visualised the Hole again and knew that it could change the face of the world in the ways that Levi described. It could change it into an awful place, where the fear of death paled in comparison to the fear of not earning enough money to buy an afterlife. His were not the ravings of a drunken mad man, she concluded, everything he'd said was likely to come true because of that Hole.

Iman had been angered by Levi's speech but she'd managed to calm herself down. "The Hole my love," she said again softly. "Come and see it now, come and see it while it's quiet."

"The Hole," Levi said nodding. "Yes the Hole. It is almost time." He smiled. "At nine a.m. I'm going to make a press release that will forever change the world as we know it," he sipped his whisky this time. "Ah," he sighed nodding appreciatively. "By then, the world will officially be in my hands. Of course, it won't affect any of you because... well, to put it quite simply, by then you will all be dead."

Dot cried out as though she was in pain. Emily felt sick. Surely some part of her father wanted to save them.

Iman turned to Levi again. "We should do it now Master. It is a new dawn, a new era, a new world is emerging." Her eyes were filled with tears. "A new world, where you will be recognised as the true master of all."

Iman was holding Levi's arm but he shook it off. He was looking at Emily as though she was the Black Death. Iman realised, "Don't worry my love. She will be gone soon enough. Let us see the Hole now, while it is calm before the storm. It is something to marvel at."

Levi shoved Iman away so that she stumbled backwards into the trestle table, knocking it and everything on it over. She was shocked but stood up and recovered herself quickly.

"Soon, it will all be over for you," he snarled drunkenly at Emily. "I'll tell the press they've been wasting their time in Iraq. They'll flock here like vultures and within hours this lake will be known all over the world: this lake, this Hole, and me," he sounded as though he was trying to convince himself.

"My love we have waited long enough, perhaps we should feed it now." Iman waived her gun at the hostages, implying they were its fodder.

"Oh!" Dot quailed.

With his spare arm, PC Birkett drew Dot's head onto his shoulder. "Shush, shush, It'll be alright," he whispered confidently, wearing an expression that said otherwise.

Suddenly Levi was enamoured of Iman again, as though he'd only just noticed her. "Yes, yes," he replied, "I must see it. Of course I must."

"But it is most beautiful when it feeds. We should feed it."

"Yes," he replied thinking of Emily, "but first I want to see its darkness, I want to hear its silence, I want to feel it breathe."

"You will not be disappointed." Iman took his hand and they disappeared under the tarp together.

28

*B*ill trained Iman's gun on them. He wasn't used to holding a gun. He found it difficult with his callused hands.

"What are we going to do?" Emily appealed to the others, as though her father wasn't there. He didn't exist for her anymore, even though he had the gun.

"Yer'll do as yer told," Bill growled. He was edging closer towards the tarpaulin that was separating the cabin from the pontoon. He was trying to listen to the two lovers behind it.

"Wur gonna' gerr' ourselves out of 'ere, before they do away wi' us that's what wur gonna' do." PC Birkett whispered but Bill heard him.

"What's that yer sayin? Mark my words, yer goin' nowhere, not in this life any road," he was snarling and waiving the gun at them.

Emily could see that Bill was in a dangerous mood. She'd seen him that way before, when he'd had too much to drink, as though he could see a fight in everything and wouldn't stop until he'd caused one.

"I'll teach yer ter go messin' around wi' me kids and me

wife," he continued, still dangerously waiving the gun in PC Birkett's face.

PC Birkett said nothing. He knew anything he said would inflame Bill even more.

Thomas wasn't thinking straight though, "They're gonna' kill us. Don't yer care about that? They're gonna' kill me and Em and me ma. Doesn't it bother yer one single bit? Wur yer family, yer own flesh and blood!"

"He betrayed us once before, 'course he doesn't cur," snarled Emily.

"Shurrup, shurrup the pair o' yer," Bill snapped. He was still trying to listen to Levi and Iman and his querulous children were interfering with that business.

But Thomas couldn't stop himself, "They're gonna' kill us and yer not even goin' ter try and stop it. How d'yer think yer gonna ger away wi' it? Don't yer think anyone's gonna' wonder whur we've all gone."

"Just give it a rest son wi' yer? All that side o' things is tekken care of."

Thomas felt a stab of hurt. Just exactly how long had his father been involved in the premeditated plans to murder his children? "Don't call me son, yer nothing ter me," Thomas spat.

Bill raised his arm to strike but Thomas' tears of frustration made him hesitate, "Calm down son, or I won't be responsible fer me actions."

"Call me son again and I'll drag yer down that Hole wi' me when me time comes."

Bill's face was alight with rage. "Right, I've bloody well 'ad enough!"

Thomas winced and closed his eyes ready to take the blow but the blow didn't come. Suddenly Bill was making a choking sound. Thomas opened his eyes. A boy had Bill's neck in the crook of his elbow. His other hand was on Bill's wrist trying to stop him from pointing the gun at anyone and firing it.

Jeremiah was tall and strong, he took after his father, so that even though he was young, he was able to restrain Bill temporarily. Bill was strong also though. Using his body was his job. He was a farmer. His frame, though crooked, was muscular and lean. He could wriggle out of a young boy's grip given time, not much more time.

PC Birkett's hands were over Dot's mouth, "Don't scream luv, don't scream. I'll let yer go if yer promise not ter. I need ter help the boy, I can get the key from Bill, just as long as yer promise yer won't scream."

Dot nodded, the strange boy had frightened her but she understood the urgency of the situation and the boy at least appeared to be on their side. PC Birkett let go of her mouth and hastily yanked her towards the boy and Bill. Bill was already beginning to overpower Jeremiah and was in danger of grabbing him around the throat. Even with only one arm, PC Birkett knew he could tip the balance. Fiercely, he grabbed Bill by the throat and held him fast. Bill's eyes were nearly popping, he was paralysed by PC Birkett's grip and could only make choking sounds. Jeremiah extracted the gun from Bill's fingers and tucked it into his trousers.

"Now, get key lad. Check 'is pockets."

Without saying a word, Jeremiah thrust his hands into Bill's pockets. He pulled out a small key and held it aloft.

"That's the one. Undo us then lad. Mekk it quick." PC Birkett was beginning to lose his grip. Bill had come too from the shock and now had both his hands clenched tightly around PC Birkett's wrist, trying to yank it away from his throat. Jeremiah managed to undo the handcuffs. PC Birkett and Dot were free from each other at last.

Suddenly PC Birkett clenched his free hand around Bill's throat as well. "I'm gonna' wring yer bleedin' neck," he snarled.

"You...wouldn't...dare," Bill choked.

But PC Birkett looked dangerous all of a sudden. "'Ere lad, 'andcuff 'im wi' yer?"

Jeremiah did as he was told. Bill was handcuffed and then tied to a chair.

"Dot yer not gonna' let 'em do this ter us are yer?" Bill appealed to his tired and terrified wife.

Dot handed Jeremiah the dirty and soggy belt of her woollen dressing gown. "'Ere, shut 'im up wi' this will yer?" she snapped.

Jeremiah obliged, gagging Bill with the filthy wet belt.

Shae-nae suddenly appeared under the tarpaulin and set to untying Thomas, finishing what she had started earlier.

"We 'eard everyfin'," she said. "We 'eard all about the Hole and everyfin'."

"Just keep untyin' us," said Thomas. "Do it quick."

"When I wos shot, I didn't go off ta some place wiv fluffy clouds an' angels, I went ta some 'orrible place. It wos cold an' dark and it stank. It ain't na picnic dahn that 'Ole I'm tellin' ya. I dahn't care 'ow rich ya' are."

PC Birkett came towards her, moved by the strange wildness about her, saddened by her look of neglect, as though nobody had ever cared for her.

"What's this?" he said, staring in disbelief into her keen eyes and noticing the lean, earnest face they were set into.

"She's bin thur before Mr Birkett." said Thomas "Some men came lookin' fer 'er and shot 'er in't head."

"Cos they wos afraid 'o me. Look, I've got one o' them scars," she stuck out her tongue and slightly further back than her piercing, was the scar; less gnarled than Levi's but just as distinct.

PC Birkett stared at her. She was a child unlike others, wild and grey beyond dirt. She was thin, yet strong and her face was knowing beyond ordinary life experience. She looked sad, he thought. "And you," he said turning to Jeremiah, "I saw yer out in't snow, I didn't believe us own eyes."

Jeremiah was nodding. He understood. "I'm sorry I hurt you," he said. "I thought you were from that place. I thought you were going to kill me."

"Ferget it lad. D'yer 'ave a scar too?"

Jeremiah nodded and stuck out his tongue.

PC Birkett nodded, he was beginning to understand.

Jeremiah was helping to untie Emily's ankles now, as PC Birkett freed her wrists.

"Shae-nae and I were both murdered. Don't ask me how we ended up back here. We just did. We followed some light and we ended up here."

Emily was free now and in her mother's arms.

PC Birkett helped Thomas up and began ushering everyone towards the tarpaulin flap that led back to the landing stage and to freedom. They were almost free when a blood curdling scream rent the air.

"Shae-nae!" Jeremiah ran back to her.

Emily followed, she knew that Levi and Iman must have heard the girl scream but she could not leave her doubled over in agony and unable to help herself.

Shae-nae's pain came again in a huge wave that forced her to her knees. That's when the shadow crept out from the dark corner and began to stalk her.

"What in God's name is that?" cried PC Birkett.

"We've got to help her, it's gonna' take her." Jeremiah wheeled around, appealing to them all. He knew the dilemma they all faced. If they stayed to help it would all be over for them, but if they went the girl had no chance. They could do nothing else but help. No one could find it within themselves to leave.

"Ere 'elp er to the chair." PC Birkett said, taking control. The girl's body was nothing to his large frame. He sat her on the chair and held her protectively as she buckled and writhed in pain. He still had Shae-nae's shoulders when her weakened body began to fade.

"Ere what the…" PC Birkett was looking at the invisible spot where the girl should be. He could still feel her solid mass in his hands, he could still feel her struggle as she writhed against her pain, but he could not see even see so much as a hair on her head.

"What the hell is going on in here?" roared Levi, as he loomed back into the cabin, pointing his gun at everyone in turn. He looked from Bill, tied up on the chair, to PC Birkett leaning over the empty chair, and was confused. He didn't see Jeremiah slip back under the tarp, or Dot nip out the flap at the front.

"What the hell d'you think your doing?" he snarled waving the gun at PC Birkett. "Get away from that chair." He didn't like the way PC Birkett was crouched over it, as though he was holding something, something that Levi could not see. PC Birkett raised both his hands and backed away.

"Get this lot tied up again will you," he barked at Iman, "How in the hell did they manage to get out?"

"He must have helped them," Iman pointed at Bill.

Levi walked over to Bill. "And this is the thanks you get for helping them, huh? See what happens when you keep changing sides?" Bill was shaking his head furiously but Levi took no notice. "I don't know which goddamned one of you I should feed to that Hole of mine first. I can't decide between you," he waived the gun under Bill's nose, while Bill shook his head furiously, "or you," he pointed at Emily.

Suddenly, another cry came from the empty chair and it tipped over.

"Who the… what the hell…" Levi fired his gun into the empty chair.

"No!" cried Emily, as another terrifying scream rent the air.

Levi continued pointing the gun at the chair where the scream had come from. He was afraid as he watched the chair jumping about, as though something invisible was bumping it; and then he saw a dark shadow sneaking towards the chair, growing darker and becoming more solid as it got closer.

"Jesus!" he gasped.

"Look at that thing. It is of the Hole." Iman said. "It is looking for something."

Levi was rattled. He fired again, this time at the shadow, but the shadow appeared unharmed, if anything it appeared to grow stronger from the shot. The shadow thickened and came closer. Suddenly its grotesque features were clearly visible. It was sniffing the air and licking its lips, as it approached the blood that was pouring down from the empty chair and growing into a pool on the floor.

29

"No!" cried Emily running forwards and kicking the creature back to its corner.

The sprite was not beaten by Emily's assault though and it re-emerged from shadow, slinking towards the chair like a suspicious cat, until it was upon the blood and lapping it up like milk.

"I'm dyin'," Shae-nae gasped. "It's consumin' me."

"It is a girl!" Iman said incredulously. "There is somebody on the chair, someone we cannot see. You shot a girl!" Iman was smiling, marvelling at the great power the Hole must have to conjure up such things.

"Yer killed 'er again. Yer murderin'…"

Emily ran at Iman. Restraining her anger for another second was impossible. She tried to claw at Iman's face but the taller, stronger woman got her wrists instead. They tussled for a while but Emily was no match for the cold, brutal woman. Swiftly letting go of one of Emily's wrists, Iman slapped her across the face for the second time that night. Emily crashed to the floor next to the empty chair and briefly saw Shae-nae's delicate form, as though it was shrouded in mist. Her pale, ghostly eyes were looking into

Emily's and her expression was gritty, determined, telling Emily to be the same.

"Get up!" Iman grabbed Emily's hair and pulled her away from Shae-nae. "You are going to be first."

In a furious rage and still dragging Emily by her hair, Iman lifted the tarp towards the Hole. "Levi, get a grip," she hissed. But Levi was not responding. Iman yanked Emily towards him. "Levi!" she snapped. But he was still staring at the sprite as it smothered the chair, searching for more blood.

Iman whacked Levi hard across the face. It was a measured, calculated and immense whack. He came to and grabbed her throat angrily.

"At last!" she said happily, despite the pressure on her throat, "Come."

He let go of her then and pointed his gun at PC Birkett and Thomas. "Where's the woman?" he asked suddenly.

Iman wheeled around. "What?"

Bill was nodding his head furiously towards the exit. Emily turned around. Her mother had gone. Her heart raced with excitement.

"Goddamn it!" shrieked Levi. "Untie that idiot and send him after her. For chrissakes she could ruin everything."

"Do not panic. She can not get far in this weather. Bill will catch her."

Iman untied Bill and handed him the knife she'd taken from Emily. He wanted to say something, he wanted to explain but she wouldn't let him she just wanted him to go.

"Move," Levi boomed. "Dead or alive, just make sure you bring her back here quickly."

Bill nodded and left.

Iman cruelly yanked Emily through the tarp by her hair. The others followed, obeying Levi's gun. Emily could see nothing at first when she stepped through the heavy flap of tarp but she could sense the Hole. She could feel its terrible power tempting her and consuming the air around her, so that she felt as though she were suffocating.

A lamp was lit, then another. Now Emily could see it. Its infinite depths made her dizzy. The oppressive body of water swirling around it was hypnotising and what power was holding back all those tonnes of water? Some power from another universe, some power beyond known science. But the blackness had changed since she last stood over it. It was breathing this time, as though it was alive, as though the blackness itself was swirling around and around inside it. One difference she could be sure of though was the pinprick of white light in its depths. That had not been there before and it was coming closer.

Levi pointed his gun at Emily. "I don't know what those things are that you've conjured up..."

"I've conjured up! You conjured them up," hissed Emily. "You conjured them up when yer killed that girl and yer own son! Well now they're back, just like Katchua's children came back. Yer didn't think of that did yer? Yer should'a known yer couldn't get rid o' them that easily."

"Shut it!" snapped Levi, firing a shot in temper through the tarp and into the night sky. Then he turned back to Emily, "Where is he?"

"He escaped," Emily replied triumphantly.

Levi paled. "Goddamn it. Did you hear that?" He turned to Iman. "Where the hell has your gun gone?" there were beads of sweat on his forehead. He was rattled.

Iman didn't know what to say. "I gave it to Bill, he must have…"

Levi wasn't listening to her excuses though; his head was spinning as his thoughts turned to his dead son. "No wait, he was dying in the woods back there. He must be dead by now, that thing was all over him." Levi seemed to get taller as the relief flooded him.

Iman placed a hand on his arm. "You saw him in the woods?" she asked gently.

"No, I heard him, he was dying, he sounded as though he was in agony. That thing, like the one all over that girl out there, there was one of them all over him too. You," he pointed his gun at Emily, he seemed in a hurry all of a sudden, "get over there. Get around the Hole until you're facing us."

Emily moved round the Hole, feeling at any moment that she might lose her balance and fall in. She stopped when she was facing Levi across the infinite depths of the divide.

"Stand closer to the edge," he ordered.

Emily took a step closer. She began to feel weightless and faint.

"It's up to you how you do it," he said. "I'm gonna' count to three, you can either jump in before I shoot you, or fall in after. I don't care which, just so long as you end up down the Hole."

Emily swayed over the edge of the Hole. So this was it, this was the night she would die after all, it just wasn't going to be on Scar Fell, it was going to be in the depths of something that made Scar Fell seem like a dot. She was going to die in the infinite depths of this Hole from another universe, possibly even another time. It was the scariest way to die that she could imagine.

The swirling light was coming up out of the Hole. Tendrils were reaching up over the edge.

"It is beautiful," gasped Iman.

The tendrils began to sneak towards Emily's ankles, wrapping around them and then spiralling up her body like serpents made of gossamer, until they reached her hair. The tendrils of light played with her hair, lifting it and twirling it, as though the light itself understood that even her hair was precious. Emily quailed and swayed dangerously. She closed her eyes, fearful of the warm tendrils embracing her. She couldn't look at Thomas, she couldn't bear to see his face so tragic and afraid for her.

"One…" Levi started his countdown.

"No! Yer can't do it ter her, please…" Thomas pleaded, trying to get to Levi but Iman held him back.

"Two…" Levi continued, ignoring him.

"Oh please," sobbed Thomas on his knees, his hands were laced together, he was begging.

Emily was no longer aware of her surroundings, she didn't hear Levi counting or Thomas pleading, she was under a spell. Her time had come and she was ready to embrace it.

*

Jeremiah crouched behind the tarp listening. He had to act fast. Emily's time was almost up. He climbed under the tarp into the dark shadows and crawled across the boards slowly, until, like an apparition, he appeared beside Emily. He watched his father's expression change.

"What the?" Levi said, staring at his son with stupefaction. Jeremiah had Iman's gun in his hand. It was trained on his father. Father and son stood across the Hole each pointing a gun at the other.

"You!" Levi gasped. "But you're…"

"Dead!" Jeremiah finished his sentence for him. "You forgot about this." Jeremiah stuck out his tongue, revealing the scar. "Don't 'demon' children belong to both worlds?" Seeing his father unnerved made him feel strong… until he felt the pains again that is. Jeremiah coughed and doubled up as though someone had kicked him in the ribs. He recovered himself quickly and managed to keep the gun pointing at his father but the pain came again, and then again, "Not now… *Please*!" he gasped.

Levi smirked when he saw the shadow sneaking up behind his son. He understood what the shadow meant. He knew the other one was feeding from the girl, taking her spirit, taking her soul, taking her body back to that place. He knew the same would happen to his son. "You're dying," he said smugly, "just like that girl. That thing has come to take you back."

"It is true," said Jeremiah trying not to flinch, "but I don't intend to go back with it alone."

"Oh, you won't be alone," laughed Levi. *"Three!"*

BANG! BANG!

Jeremiah fell down on his knees, clutching a bloody wound in his stomach. It didn't really hurt, not so much as the cramps but he knew it weakened him further. Emily had gone. A patch of blood from her bullet wound was smeared on the floorboards where she'd fallen before sliding into the Hole. Jeremiah's sprite was upon him now smothering him; it was going to take him back down the Hole...

BANG!

Jeremiah didn't know where the third shot had come from, or who, if anyone was hit; all he knew was that his father's laughter was silenced and he felt as though he was falling.

30

Jeremiah knew he was leaving the world again. A vague feeling of failure perturbed him but he remembered less and less what had happened. He was falling now, not fast and dramatically so that his heart raced and made him afraid, but slowly and softly as though the air was a cradle, lowering him gently. He knew the sprite was still there by his side and he could see the castle. Dark feelings of foreboding flooded over him but they kept ebbing and flowing like the tide, until eventually he couldn't remember the point at which they disappeared. He knew he was back in that place. It was dark and snowy and by now he could see the castle in the distance. He saw Shae-nae in the distance too. He couldn't remember why she was there. She was talking to a woman. The woman had her back to him but she seemed familiar somehow.

Jeremiah had stopped floating and was standing on the ground still looking at the woman and trying to place her, when he realised there was a body lying on the cold snowy ground next to him. It was Emily. She was clutching her belly, although her blood had stopped flowing now. She was still unconscious, or drugged, he could not tell which.

She would be afraid when she came to, just as he had been.

A woman suddenly came towards him. It was the same woman who had been talking to Shae-nae. He was sure he knew her. The woman suddenly reached out and pulled him towards her, holding him tightly. He didn't push her off. He didn't want to. She was warm: he knew her.

"Son," she said.

Jeremiah had never known his mother despite yearning for her all his life.

"My son, I knew you would come to me again."

Jeremiah drank in the scent of her, the sound of her voice, the feel of her soft bosom against his cheek, rising and falling with her breath.

"Mother!" he gasped, but it was all he could say.

"Son, you must listen to me for we will be parted again soon."

"No, no, I don't want to go…".

"Listen!" her voice was commanding. She took his shoulders and looked deep into his eyes. Her eyes were like his father's, green and all piercing, although she was not dark like him. "You never knew me in this life because I died when you were born, and lived as another."

"But…"

"I know I know, your father told you I died in a car crash. That was because he couldn't bring himself to tell you the truth. The truth, the sadness of it corrupted him somehow and ate away at him. He never spoke the truth about my death to anyone. Only the doctors knew. I died in childbirth."

"What! I don't understand…"

"Listen Jeremiah, you must listen, there is a lot to take in and very little time. I died giving birth to your twin brother. He died too. There were complications, he had no oxygen, he…" She closed her eyes for a moment and composed herself.

"I had a brother!" Jeremiah gasped.

"My son, do not be sad, you did not know me in this life but we knew each other once before. I lived as Katchua and you were my son Jiayoulu."

Jeremiah wept: "I had a brother."

"Jeremiah, look at me." Her features seemed to alter slightly, as though she was more than one woman, although the changes were so subtle Jeremiah believed he was imagining it. He stopped crying and looked into her eyes. Her expression was serious. "Jeremiah, you *do* have a brother. He lives as another. Do you understand me? Your twin brother lives."

Jeremiah stared at her with moist eyes. "But it's too late."

His mother's face was strong. "It's never too late Jeremiah, he is closer than you think, much closer. The others have not thought about him, they thought he did not count because he was not alive when he was born. But he was alive in my womb and his spirit was created the moment he was conceived. His spirit and his soul live on in another. He does not bear a scar… The punishments were metered out long after he was gone. Go back. Go back at once, he will save you."

Suddenly her eyes were wide and she gasped as though she had just received a blow. Jeremiah was afraid, until she smiled up into the dark night. Then, still smiling, she looked back at Jeremiah. "Go," she said again. "My son has already saved you."

"What about Shae-nae?"

"You will see," was all she would say.

"And Emily?"

Katchua looked at Emily lying on the ground. "She must stay with me," she said impassively. "She is waiting for something."

He tried to feel worried about Emily but he couldn't. Then his sprite began to pull him back towards the light, as though they were wading through the sea.

31

*T*homas didn't know where his strength had suddenly come from. He'd dived for Jeremiah's gun, aimed and fired without thinking. It had been instinct, an instinct based on survival; an instinct driven by anger as he'd watched his sister buckle from the shot and fall into the Hole. That smug expression of Levi's had to be wiped off his face. How dare he look like that after killing Emily? The gun was still smoking. He was pointing it at Iman now.

Iman could see that Thomas was still trembling but she could see that he was capable of using the gun again. Something about him was changed: his expression was hard, determined. Levi's gun was right there on the boards, just within reach, he'd dropped it when the boy had shot him. She could get it but... the boy... the way the light from the Hole lit up his face...it didn't just make him look stronger and more powerful, it made him look unafraid. She couldn't afford to be rash.

"Throw me the pendant," he ordered.

Iman froze hoping she'd misheard him. The pendant was to be her life line in the event of her death. She'd always had that in mind, giving it up was not an option. But she hadn't misheard.

"Throw me the pendant," Thomas said again.

Iman darted a look at Levi's gun.

"Don't even think about it," said Thomas, pointing the gun at her more intently.

Iman smiled suddenly and pulled the pendant out of her blouse. The blinding light from it filled the room, instantly blinding everyone. Quickly, she crouched down and felt for the gun on the boards. She found it. Holding the gun firmly in one hand, she tucked the pendant back inside her blouse with the other. It seemed the pendant was to save her from death itself.

"Well, well," she said smugly, "you did not really think I would give it to you just like that did you?" Now she had a gun and she was pointing it at Thomas.

But Thomas didn't relinquish his hold on his gun. He wasn't even shaken. It was as though he didn't care whether he lived or died.

"Put the gun down boy," Iman ordered.

Thomas just stared at her stonily, until a strange change came over him. His face seemed to cloud and his mouth began to stretch open, as though it was moving independently of him, as though he had no control over it. He looked grotesque. Then Thomas began to make crying noises. The crying was becoming more and more distressed. The crying was that of a new born baby.

"What the…Shut up! Shut up making that noise. What are you doing? Stop it, stop it at once." Iman stepped back shocked. The boy was possessed. It made her afraid, so she pulled the trigger of the gun.

There was a click, Thomas fell silent and his face returned to normal. He was staring at Iman's gun solemnly.

Iman pulled the trigger again but it just kept making the same impotent clicking noise. The chamber was empty.

Thomas raised his gun. He took aim. Iman flinched.

BANG!

Thomas' chamber wasn't empty and the barrel of his gun was smoking again.

Levi cried out in pain again when Iman fell on top of him. She was wounded, and she was weak but the wound was not fatal. Sobbing, Iman placed her forehead on Levi's. Her hair, like black velvet, shrouded them: privacy for two lovers in their parting moments. Levi gasped in pain again and Iman stroked his face as her tears washed over him. She could feel the warmth of her blood oozing between them. There was a lot, perhaps her injures were more serious. She felt light headed but she lifted her head up anyway. "I know who you are," she hissed staring at Thomas with pure hatred but she did not explain herself.

Suddenly, the tarpaulin behind her began to bulge inwards. Something was backing towards them from underneath the tarp. It was a sprite, snuffling heavily and wetly, as it dragged its heavy load along with it. It was dragging the body of Shae-nae.

Nobody was looking at the Hole now, everybody was looking at the hideous sprite and the dead body of the girl. Nobody noticed the two thin tendrils of light dancing up out of the Hole, like two beautiful perfect partners.

Iman cried out again but this time it was in disgust, as the sprite struggled with Shae-nae's motionless body. It was all going so wrong. The Hole and anything associated with it had lost its appeal. Iman rolled off Levi's body. There was a burning pain in her chest and she knew if she didn't act now she wouldn't be able to. She was loosing a lot of blood and she was already feeling weak but she could still find the strength.

"Don't go," Levi gasped, grabbing her arm firmly.

Iman winced. "Do not be afraid my love, it is just for a second," and she tried to wriggle free but Levi wouldn't let go.

"I don't want to be alone," he gasped.

There was a sudden rumble like thunder. The boards trembled beneath them. The tendrils of light climbed higher, continuing to dance together, as though nothing else existed but them. Then there was another sound coming from the Hole, the sound of snuffling and wet heavy breathing, and such a terrible stench! There was a terrible belch of sulphurous gas and then Jeremiah's body landed awkwardly on the boards beside Thomas, coughed up out of the Hole by the thing breathing heavily below its rim. Elongated fingers with rotten flesh suddenly appeared and gripped the rim. The breathing became heavier as Jeremiah's sprite began to drag itself up out of the Hole.

Shae-nae's sprite was close but had paused to watch the other sprite emerge. Then it looked back at Shae-nae's body. It paused momentarily, before climbing on top of her and smothering her with its foul, stinking flesh. Iman shuddered, and laid her head back on the boards, relieved that it wasn't coming for her. It was taking the girl. It wanted the girl, she reminded herself with relief. If only Levi would let go of her arm so that she could get away.

The sprite's slimy skin was vaguely transparent. Shae-nae's dark form could be seen beneath it. A black oily lump in its deformed chest beat ever more ferociously as its fingers touched Shae-nae's stomach, just gently at first. Then it lifted her t-shirt and its fingers scrabbled about on her bare flesh like spiders.

From underneath the t-shirt came the sound of tearing flesh. The sprite's fingers were ripping into her flesh and delving inside her body. As though satisfied that it had found something, some part of her that it wanted, it ducked its foul fat head underneath her shirt as well, and the mass of its head and arms unfeasibly disappeared beneath it. The rest of its slimy body followed, sliding underneath her shirt like some vast alien reptile until its whole body was gone inside her.

Shae-nae's skin bulged up underneath her t-shirt and

her flesh began to ripple all over. The sprite was inside her, possessing her. Suddenly Shae-nae's soft body became rigid. Her arms, legs and fingers were thrust out like poles and her head flew backwards, eyes suddenly wide open, yet dead and unseeing. Shae-nae's body jumped off the boards as though she was being electrocuted. It jumped again and again. Then it stopped.

The sprite was coming out from under her t-shirt, sliming out, growing fat and engorged as it re-emerged, until it was beside her again. Shae-nae's chest was rising and falling with each intake and out take of breath, but nobody noticed that just yet.

"Levi please," Iman begged, trying to wriggle free from his grip, especially now that the sprite was back again and closer than she would like. She darted a look across the Hole where the other sprite was climbing all over Jeremiah. The boy's sprite was going to do the same thing, she thought, as she watched it disappear under his sweater.

"Let go of me, goddamn it!" Iman screamed at Levi, "Let go you idiot!"

As though it had not been aware of her before, Shae-nae's sprite turned and glared at her with its red eyes. Iman trembled. Its gaze was purposeful, as though it had found something that it prized very highly.

Levi sounded weak when he spoke again. "I'm dying Iman. I'm afraid."

But Iman wasn't listening. She could not take her eyes

off the sprite. It looked like the girl suddenly, the dead girl, but grey and bloated and... it had a bullet hole in its head and gut. The dead girl suddenly began to splutter. Iman lifted her head from the boards again and looked beyond the sprite at the girl. She was gasping for breath and sitting up, now she was wiping all that slime off her, the slime that the creature had covered her with. Where had her bullet wounds gone? How could she be alive after everything?

Suddenly Jeremiah too began to splutter. He coughed up the sprite slime that had been covering him. He opened his eyes and he was staring, puzzled. He looked around him, at Thomas, at Levi and Iman lying on the floor bleeding. His sprite was beside him, its form engorged just like Shae-nae's sprite. Oily black blood was seeping from its stomach. Its shoulder was crooked and its neck twisted at an unnatural angle.

"No!" cried Levi. "This cannot be happening!"

Jeremiah's sprite began skulking towards Levi.

Iman wasn't thinking of anyone but herself. She'd seen enough, she needed to get away. The gun was gone. She had no weapons. She was going to have to play clever if she wanted to survive and Levi... *well he could go to Hell!*

"I don't want to die," he moaned again.

Iman shuddered. He disgusted her in his dying moments. He was acting like a little baby.

"I don't want to die alone Iman," he still had hold of her arm.

"You won't be alone darling. I'll get help but you will have to let me go first…my love."

Levi reached over to her and stroked her face with his spare hand. He let go of her arm but to her surprise he grabbed a great trestle of her magnificent hair.

"I won't be alone because you'll come with me won't you…my love." The last two words hobbled from his mouth unnaturally. He'd never said them before: he didn't mean them now. And the words that Iman longed to hear up until now chilled her heart because she could see the emptiness in them and the reason behind them. He wanted to take her with him. He took her for a fool. If he'd loved her before she might have sacrificed herself… but not now, it was too late now. No, she would not die for him. The Hole frightened her too.

Both sprites were coming towards them now, sidling up to them like cats, deliciously curious of a new toy.

"Let me go, or so help me I'll put you out of your misery right now," Iman threatened coldly, placing her hands around his throat and trying to ignore the sprites getting closer and the bright light coming up out of the Hole again.

"You wouldn't dare," choked Levi.

"Dare…" she pretended to think, "or die. Oh, I think I dare. It's not as though I haven't killed before… *my love,* she mocked."

"You're not strong enough," he mocked.

"Not strong enough to choke the breath out of a dying man when I've choked the breath out of healthy men many times over. You know where I trained," she replied simply. She was bluffing, but he didn't know that. He paused unsure. "Test me," she sneered, "Or let go of me."

Levi let go of her hair. Iman smiled marvelling at the power of lies. Satisfied, she let go of his neck but her smile and her triumph began to dissolve quickly. The sprite was still coming for her.

Iman tried to get up but the searing pain in her chest prevented her. Shae-nae's sprite stood over Iman. The stench of rotten flesh seeping from its folds of skin was overpowering as its viscous body began to climb on top of her feet, sliming up her legs towards her torso. She was screaming now, screaming as though she was being butchered alive. It made no difference, the sprite just glided over her until all but her face was covered. The sprite's red eyes glowed with excitement as Iman screamed for the last time, then it clamped its stinking, viscous face to hers, until she was engulfed.

Jeremiah shuddered as he looked at his sprite's broken shoulder and the bullet wound in its gut. Its head was slightly crushed on one side, as though from the impact of a car. "It absorbed my shot for me, it absorbed my death. It's been protecting me," he gasped. Jeremiah looked at his terrified father writhing in pain on the boards. He had wanted to see his father like this, dreamed of it, but it gave him no pleasure now.

Levi was screaming: "No, no, no!" knowing what Jeremiah's sprite was coming to do to him. Its long arms and grey hands were reaching out towards him, the oily black lump in its chest was beating ferociously as it climbed upon him and began to suck the remaining life out of him, by clamping its putrid face to his. Suddenly the creature's broken shoulder began to bulge, as though it were growing another head. Stretching and squeezing through its putrid flesh was the image of Levi's terrified face, frozen with fear.

The two dancing tendrils of light were not alone now. There were hundreds more delicate tendrils, just reaching up out of the Hole. The dancing pair were up over the edge and gliding across the boards like golden serpents. Each of the tendrils began to coil its length around an engorged sprite. At their touch, the sprites seemed to melt and sink down to the floor like quicksilver. The golden tendrils of light began to drag the sprite's silvery mass over the edge and down into the Hole. Iman's pendant lay on the floor, its brightness dulled by a thick layer of sprite slime.

Now the light from the Hole was becoming unstable. Its great tendrils began swishing about like loose, live electricity cables. They were flailing wildly around, trying to grab, snap and lasso the air. One snapped near PC Birkett.

"Come on, we've got ter get out o' 'ere."

"But what about Em?" cried Thomas."

"She's gone lad. This thing is bigger than us. It came fer her, it's got her now."

"No, she can't be."

"Thomas, she's dead. Come on we've got ter ger outta 'ere."

PC Birkett tried to grab Thomas' arm but he ducked and legged it round the Hole.

"Thomas, what yer…?"

Thomas squinted against the bright coils of condensed light as he wiped the slime from Iman's pendant and then he hurled it down the Hole.

"What are you doing?" screamed Jeremiah, as he held open the flap of tarpaulin.

"Helping… hoping. I don't know," Thomas cried in answer.

"Come on. We need to get out of here," urged Jeremiah more gently.

32

"*R*un!" Shae-nae screamed at Thomas and Jeremiah. "It's abaht ta explode."

Great spires of light began shooting out of the Hole in all directions.

"Oh, ruddy 'ell, this thing's gonna' blow!" shouted PC Birkett, shoving them all along faster. Just as they jumped onto the frozen bank, the light exploded through the roof of the tarpaulin, lifting it, as though it were no more than a tissue. The pontoon and the jetty shook and great planks of wood began falling off them and splashing into the water below. Big supporting beams crashed down into the lake, until half the jetty was gone.

They were on the beach, heading for the woods when the rest of the pontoon crashed down and the lake's waters began to rise from the massive explosion that was being created inside the Hole. They were running up the hill, through the woods and towards the witch tree, where Thomas had first hidden from Levi all those hours ago. They weren't hiding this time though, they were watching: watching the water rise up and come towards them; watching the drill fall over, its heavy, dinosaur like head crashing into the lake; watching the pontoon being smashed up, as though it was made of matchsticks; but most incredible of all was the light. More great bolts of light ripped up out of the unmasked Hole and charged up to the stars.

The surging water began to retreat, picking up broken pieces of pontoon and crashing them together, as though sinking a boat on high seas. There was another explosive crack. The Hole appeared to be spinning and widening out across the lake. Even from the safe distance of the witch tree, the earth felt as though it was crumbling beneath them. Another crack and the drill was shunted into the lake and dragged into the maelstrom. Everything was disappearing down into the Hole, the drill, the pontoon, the tarp... a directory listing Kinsmen and Kinswomen of the United Kingdom.

The directory that Emily had found in the cottage was dancing in the maelstrom, its pages blown open in the tornado created by the spinning Hole. If they had been close enough, they would have seen the photograph of a woman, then they would have known not to trust her.

33

WPC Turner brushed the snow from her shoulders, wondering why the police station was deserted. PC Birkett must have gone out. There must have been an incident, she thought. The gas fire was on full pelt and yet it was cold. She switched it off. There was a bitter draught coming from somewhere. WPC Turner looked up to see the window above PC Birkett's desk was wide open. She closed it and then noticed the files on the floor and the papers from his desk, strewn all over the room. She had her work cut out clearing this mess up. She hung her coat up. *How long had he been gone and why did he leave the window open?*

WPC Turner closed the window and put the files back on the ledge. The papers on the floor though... she didn't know where to start with those. Eventually she was sitting patiently going through them all, turning them all the right way up, before scanning the contents and assessing the level of each paper's importance. But WPC Turner's mind wasn't on the job: she was too excited. Today was the day: the day the world would change. If only her internet connection hadn't been down, and how could she have let the battery on her satellite phone run out of power? Now she had no update, she didn't know how it was all going.

A scruffy, childishly written note amongst the pile of official papers caught her attention. WPC Turner's heart pounded when she read it. She looked around the station suddenly piecing together what had been happening. She read the note again. Her eyes lingered on the author's name. Emily Hayward. She was the one. What had she been doing here?

Suddenly there was a desperate banging on the station door. WPC Turner became anxious and afraid. Cautiously, she made her way to the door.

"Is thur anyone in thur?" came a terrified and desperate plea from the other side of the door. "Open't door! Please, fer't love o' God, if thur's someone thur, please open't door."

Damn it, thought WPC Turner. Slowly and reluctantly she opened the door.

Dot burst past her into the tiny station. "Oh, thank God," she cried. "We 'ave ter go, we have ter go now! Thur's trouble down at lake. Thur gonna' murder our Thomas and our Emily." At that Dot became choked up and she began to sob.

WPC Turner couldn't believe what she was seeing, she recognised the woman of course: it was Emily Hayward's mother, but the state she was in was something of a shock, and that coat... what was she doing wearing *that coat? What was she doing here full stop!*

"Let me just mekk things right 'ere love and I'll 'elp yer. Just give us one second will yer." WPC Turner needed time to think.

Dot nodded, swallowing dryly instead of protesting, although she wanted to protest, waiting an extra second under the circumstances would feel like torture.

WPC Turner took Emily's note into the staff kitchenette and held it over the draining board. She didn't want Dot to see it. *Well there was no sense upsetting her even more, not yet any road.* With her other hand, she flicked a lighter with her thumb. The flame ignited and she applied it to the note, letting the flames carry it down gently onto the cold dry metal. When it was no more than black ash she rinsed it into the sink with water and smiled as she watched the evidence dissolve and swirl down into the plug hole forever. Now she would take the woman and look for Bill to find out what the hell had gone wrong.

34

"**L**ook!" cried Thomas. Like the moments before a total eclipse, a bright ring of light settled peacefully on the tumultuous waters of the lake; but almost as soon as he'd said it, the ring was gone and only the darkness remained.

"It's all gone," said Thomas, pointing incredulously at the lake. "Even the drill," he added as though it was hard to believe that such a huge steel structure could disappear just as easily as a snowdrop in the sun. But the disappearance of the Hole made him feel sick. He knew he would never see Emily again.

Shae-nae wasn't looking at the lake though, she was looking up at the stars. She was thanking them. She had to direct her thanks somewhere. She had to be grateful to something for letting her see her mother again. So many painful things had been laid to rest during the encounter in that place. When Katarina explained the terrible painful sadness deep inside her that she had never been able to understand, a sadness that compelled her to self destruct, Shae-nae understood. She understood that her mother was suffering from grief, a grief born from the loss of a child in another dimension of herself, a grief deep inside the same soul that her mother shared with Katchua. Now though, Katarina understood, and she was changed. Her afterlife had changed her and brought her the peace she longed for but could never obtain in life. That peace came to Shae-nae also and Shae-nae loved her mother all over again. Now Shae-nae knew that when her time came, her mother, free from pain, would be there waiting to embrace her.

But her time had not come after all and PC Birkett said help would be on its way. They were all waiting for the woman known as WPC Turner. She was going to help them.

35

An orange line on the horizon signalled the rising of the sun. The winter night was coming to an end. First light brought with it warm tones of orange that softened the white landscape hardened by the long winter's night. Long shadows reached out and caressed the cold earth like old friends, and golden ripples decorated the lake like tinsel on a Christmas tree.

Thomas and the others didn't see Bill crouching in the long shadows of the trees. They were too busy smiling at their mother as she appeared over the brow of the hill. Dot had escaped, she was alive and well and she had brought help. Another woman was waiving and smiling at them too.

"I told yer she'd be early," PC Birkett beamed proudly. "WPC Turner's never lerrus down yet."

"Ma, Ma!" Thomas ran towards Dot, threw his arms around her and sobbed, sobbed with relief and sobbed for Emily. But at least it was over.

WPC Turner kept a polite distance from the reunion. She was looking beyond them anyway. She was looking at the centre of the lake. They couldn't see it, they were too busy hugging and fussing with each other. They couldn't see the subtle ring of light redeveloping in its centre. The policewoman sees it and as though she has some gift she looks towards the trees where Bill is hiding. She smiles and beckons him over. She is satisfied that they haven't worked out that she is one of them, but she will wait for his help anyway. She will wait for Bill to come and then they will know...